James Anthony Froude

Life and Times of Thomas Becket

James Anthony Froude

Life and Times of Thomas Becket

ISBN/EAN: 9783337059088

Printed in Europe, USA, Canada, Australia, Japan

Cover: Foto ©Raphael Reischuk / pixelio.de

More available books at **www.hansebooks.com**

THOMAS BECKET.

LIFE AND TIMES

OF

THOMAS BECKET.

BY

JAMES ANTHONY FROUDE, M. A.

NEW YORK:

SCRIBNER, ARMSTRONG AND COMPANY.

1878.

RIVERSIDE, CAMBRIDGE:

STEREOTYPED AND PRINTED BY

H. O. HOUGHTON AND COMPANY.

LIFE AND TIMES

OF

THOMAS BECKET.[1]

CHAPTER I.

AMONG the earliest efforts of the modern sacerdotal party in the Church of England was an attempt to reëstablish the memory of the martyr of Canterbury. The sacerdotal party, so far as their objects were acknowledged, aspired only to liberate the Church from bondage to the State. The choice of Becket as an object of adoration was a tacit confession of their real ambition. The theory of Becket was not that the Church had a right to self-administration, but that the Church was the supreme administrator in this world, and perhaps in the next; that the secular sword as well as the spiritual had been delivered to Peter; and that the civil power existed only as the delegate of Peter's successors. If it be true that the clergy are possessed in any real sense of supernatural powers; if the "keys," as they are called, have been actually granted to them; if through them, as the ordinary and appointed channel, the will of God is alone made known to mankind — then Becket was right, and the High Churchmen are right, and kings and cabinets ought to be superseded at once by commissions of

---

1 *Materials for the History of Thomas Becket, Archbishop of Canterbury.* Edited by James Craigie Robertson, Canon of Canterbury. Published under the direction of the Master of the Rolls. 1876.

bishops. If, on the other hand, the clergy are but like other orders of priesthoods in other ages and countries — mere human beings set apart for peculiar functions, and tempted by the nature of those functions into fantastic notions of their own consequence — then these recurring conflicts between Church and State resolve themselves into phenomena of social evolution, the common sense of mankind exerting itself to control a groundless assumption. To the student of human nature the story of such conflicts is always interesting — comedy and tragedy winding one into the other. They have furnished occasion for remarkable exhibitions of human character. And while Churchmen are raising up Becket as a brazen serpent, on which the world is to look to be healed of its incredulities, the incredulous world may look with advantage at him from its own point of view, and, if unconvinced that he was a saint, may still find instruction in a study of his actions and his fate.

We take advantage, then, of the publication of· new materials and the republication of old materials in an accessible form to draw a sketch of Becket as he appears to ourselves ; and we must commence with an attempt to reproduce the mental condition of the times in which he lived. Human nature is said to be always the same. It is no less true that human nature is continuously changing. Motives which in one age are languid and even unintelligible have been in another alive and all-powerful. To comprehend these differences, to take them up into his imagination, to keep them present before him as the key to what he reads, is the chief difficulty and the chief duty of the student of history.

Characteristic incidents, particular things which men representative of their age indisputably did, convey a clearer idea than any general description. Let the reader attend to a few transactions which occurred either in Becket's lifetime or immediately subsequent to it, in which the principal actors were persons known to himself.

We select as the first a scene at Martel near Limoges in the year 1183.   Henry Plantagenet, eldest son of Henry the Second, Prince of Wales as we should now call him, called then " the young king," for he was crowned in his father's lifetime, at that spot and in that year brought his disordered existence to an end.   His career had been wild and criminal.   He had rebelled against his father again and again; again and again he had been forgiven.   In a fit of remorse he had taken the cross, and intended to go to Jerusalem.   He forgot Jerusalem in the next temptation. He joined himself to Lewis of France, broke once more into his last and worst revolt, and carried fire and sword into Normandy.   He had hoped to bring the nobles to his side; he succeeded only in burning towns and churches, stripping shrines, and bringing general hatred on himself. Finding, we are told, that he could not injure his father as much as he had hoped to do, he chafed himself into a fever, and the fever killed him.   Feeling death to be near, he sent a message to his father begging to see him.   The old Henry, after past experience, dared not venture.   The prince (I translate literally from a contemporary chronicler) —

then called his bishops and religious men to his side.   He confessed his sins first in private, then openly to all who were present.   He was absolved.   He gave his cross to a friend to carry to the Holy Sepulchre.   Then, throwing off his soft clothing, he put on a shirt of hair, tied a rope about his neck, and said to the bishops —

" By this rope I deliver over myself, a guilty and unworthy sinner, to you the ministers of God.   Through your intercession and of his own ineffable mercy, I beseech our Lord Jesus Christ, who forgave the thief upon the cross, to have pity on my unhappy soul."

A bed of ashes had been prepared on the floor.

" Drag me," he went on, " by this rope out of this bed, and lay me on the ashes."

The bishop did so.   They placed at his head and at his feet two large square stones, and so he died.

There is one aspect of the twelfth century — the darkest crimes and the most real superstition side by side coexisting in the same character.

Turn from Martel to Oxford, and go back seventeen years. Men who had so little pity on themselves were as pitiless to others. We quote from Stowe. The story is authenticated by contemporary chroniclers.

1166. There came into England thirty Germans, as well men as women, who called themselves Publicans. Their head and ruler, named Gerardus, was somewhat learned; the residue very rude. They denied matrimony and the sacraments of baptism and the Lord's Supper, with other articles. They being apprehended, the king caused a council to be called at Oxford, where the said Gerard answered for all his fellows, who being pressed with Scripture answered concerning their faith as they had been taught, and would not dispute thereof. After they could by no means be brought from their errors, the bishop gave sentence against them, and the king commanded that they should be marked with a hot iron in the forehead and whipped, and that no man should succor them with house-room or otherwise. They took their punishment gladly, their captain going before them singing, "Blessed are ye when men hate you." They were marked both in the forehead and the chin. Thus being whipped and thrust out in winter, they died with cold, no man relieving them.

To the bishops of Normandy Henry Plantagenet handed the rope to drag him to his death-bed of ashes. Under sentence from the bishops of England these German heretics were left to a fate more piteous than the stake. The privilege and authority of bishops and clergy was Becket's plea for convulsing Europe. What were the bishops and clergy like themselves? We will look at the bishops assembled at the Council of Westminster in the year 1176. Cardinal Hugezun had come as legate from Rome. The council was attended by the two archbishops, each accompanied by his suffragans, the abbots, priors, and clergy of his province. Before business began, there arose *dira lis et contentio,* a dreadful strife and contention between these high personages as to which archbishop should sit on the cardinal's right hand. Richard of Canterbury said the right was with him. Roger of York said the right was with him. Words turned to blows. The monks of Canterbury, zealous for their master, rushed upon the Archbishop of York, flung him down, kicked him, and danced upon him till he was almost dead. The cardinal wrung his hands, and charged the Archbishop of Canterbury with having set them on. The Archbishop of York made his way, bruised and bleeding, to the king. Both parties in the first heat appealed to the pope. Canterbury on second thoughts repented, went privately to the cardinal, and bribed him to silence. The appeal was withdrawn, the affair dropped, and the council went on with its work.

So much for the bishops. We may add that Becket's friend John of Salisbury accuses the Archbishop of York, on common notoriety, of having committed the most infamous of crimes, and of having murdered the partners of his guilt to conceal it.[1]

As to the inferior clergy, it might be enough to quote the language used about them at the conference at Montmiraux in 1169, where their general character was said to be atrocious, a great number of them being church-robbers, adulterers, highwaymen, thieves, ravishers of virgins, incendiaries, and murderers.[2] For special illustration we take a visitation of St. Augustine's Abbey at Canterbury in the year 1173, undertaken by the pope's order. The visitors reported not only that the abbot was corrupt, extravagant, and tyrannical, but that he had more children than the patriarchs, in one village as many as ten or twelve bastards.

---

[1] John of Salisbury to the Archbishop of Sens, 1171. The Archbishop of York is spoken of under the name of Caiaphas.

[2] "Quum tamen clerici immundissimi et atrocissimi sunt, utpote qui ex magnâ parte sacrilegi, adulteri. prædones, fures, raptores virginum, incendiarii et homicidæ sunt." — John of Salisbury to the Bishop of Exeter. Letters, 1169.

"*Velut equus hinnit in fœminas,*' they said, "adeo impudens ut libidinem nisi quam publicaverit voluptuosam esse non reputet. Matres et earundem filias incestat pariter. For-nicationis abusum comparat necessitati." This precious ab-bot was the host and entertainer of the four knights when they came to Canterbury.

From separate pictures we pass to a sketch of the condi-tion of the Church of England written by a monk of Christ Church, Canterbury, a contemporary of Becket, when the impression of the martyrdom was fresh, and miracles were worked by his relics every day under the writer's eyes. The monk's name was Nigellus. He was precentor of the cathedral. His opinion of the wonders of which he was the witness may be inferred from the shrug of the shoulders with which, after describing the disorders of the times, he says that they were but natural, for the age of miracles was past. In reading him we feel that we are looking on the old England through an extremely keen pair of eyes. We discern too, perhaps, that he was a clever fellow, constitu-tionally a satirist, and disappointed of promotion, and we make the necessary allowances. Two of his works survive, one in verse, the other in serious prose.

The poem, which is called *Speculum Stultorum* ("'The Looking-Glass of Fools") contains the adventures of a monk who leaves his cloister to better his fortunes. The monk is introduced under the symbolic disguise of an ass. His ambition is to grow a longer tail, and he wanders un-successfully over Europe, meeting as many misfortunes as Don Quixote, in pursuit of his object. Finally he arrives at Paris, where he resolves to remain and study, that at all events he may write after his name *magister artium.* The seven years' course being finished, he speculates on his fut-ure career. He decides on the whole that he will be a bishop, and pictures to himself the delight of his mother when she sees him in his pontificals. Sadly, however, he

soon remembers that bishops were not made of such stuff
as learned members of the universities. Bishops were born
in barons' castles, and named as children to the sees which
they were to occupy. "Little Bobby" and "little Willy"
were carried to Rome in their nurses' arms before they
could speak or walk, to have the keys of heaven committed
to them. So young were they sometimes that a wit said
once that it could not be told whether the bishop elect was a
boy or a girl.[1] An abbey might suit better, he thought, and
he ran over the various attractions of the different orders.
All of them were more or less loose rogues, some worse, some
better.[2] On the whole the monk-ass concluded that he
would found a new order, the rules of which should be com-
pounded of the indulgences allowed to each of the rest. The
pope would consent if approached with the proper tempta-
tions; and he was picturing to himself the delightful life
which he was thenceforth to lead, when his master found
him and cudgelled him back to the stable.

More instructive, if less amusing, is the prose treatise
Contra Curiales et Officiales clericos ("Against Clerical
Courtiers and Officials"), dedicated to De Longchamp,
Bishop of Ely, Cœur de Lion's chancellor, who was left in

[1] " Ante prius patrem primum matremque vocare
       Quam sciat, aut possit stare vel ire pedes,
     Suscipit ecclesiæ claves animasque regendas.
       In cunis positus dummodo vagit adhuc
     Cum nutrice suâ, Romam Robekimus adibit,
       Quem nova sive vetus sportula tecta feret;
     Missus et in peram veniet Wilekinus in urbem,
       Curia Romana tota videbit eum.
     Impuberes pueros pastores ecclesiarum
       Vidimus effectos pontificesque sacros.
     Sic dixit quidam de quodam pontificando,
       Cum princeps regni solicitaret eum:
     'Est puer, et nondum discernere possumus utrum
       Fœmina vel mas est, et modo præsul erit.'"
           Satirical Poems of the Twelfth Century, vol. i. p. 106.

[2] " Omnes sunt fures, quocunque charactere sacro
       Signati veniant magnificentque Deum."

charge of the realm when Richard went to Palestine.   De
Longchamp's rule was brief and stormy.   It lasted long
enough, however, to induce Nigellus to appeal to him for a
reform of the Church, and to draw a picture of it which admirers of the ages and faith may profitably study.

At whatever period we get a clear view of the Church of
England, it was always in terrible need of reform.   In the
twelfth century it has been held to have been at its best.
Let us look then at the actual condition of it.

According to Nigellus, the Church benefices in England,
almost without exception, were either sold by the patrons
to the highest bidders, or were given by them to their near
relations.   The presentees entered into possession more
generally even than the bishops when children.

Infants in cradles (says Nigellus) are made archdeacons, that
out of the mouths of babes and sucklings praise may be per-
fected.   The child is still at the breast and he is a priest of the
Church.   He can bind and loose before he can speak, and has
the keys of heaven before he has the use of his understanding.
At an age when an apple is more to him than a dozen churches,
he is set to dispense the sacraments, and the only anxiety about
him is a fear that he may die.   He is sent to no school.   He is
idle and is never whipped.   He goes to Paris to be polished,
where he learns "the essentials of a gentleman's education,"
dice and dominoes, *et cætera quæ sequuntur.*   He returns to England to hawk and hunt, and would that this were the worst! but
he has the forehead of a harlot, and knows not to be ashamed.
To such persons as these a bishop without scruple commits the
charge of souls — to men who are given over to the flesh, who
rise in the morning to eat, and sit down at evening to drink,
who spend on loose women the offerings of the faithful, who do
things which make their people blush to speak of them, while
they themselves look for the Jordan to flow into their mouths,
and expect each day to hear a voice say to them, "Friend, go
up higher."

Those who had no money to buy their way with, and no
friends to help them, were obliged to study something.

Having done with Paris they would go on to Bologna, and come back knowing medicine and law and speaking pure French and Italian. Clever fellows, so furnished, contrived to rise by pushing themselves into the service of bishop or baron, to whom "they were as eyes to the blind and as feet to the lame." They managed the great man's business; they took care of his health. They went to Rome with his appeals, undertook negotiations for him in foreign courts, and were repaid in time by prebends and rectories. Others, in spite of laws of celibacy, married a patron's daughter, and got a benefice along with her. It was illegal, but the bishops winked at it. Others made interest at Rome with the cardinals, and by them were recommended home. Others contrived to be of use to the king. Once on the road to preferment the ascent was easy. The lucky ones, not content with a church or two, would have a benefice in every diocese in England, and would lie, cheat, "forget God, and not remember man." Their first gains were spent in bribes to purchase more, and nothing could satisfy them. Fifteen or twenty rectories were not enough without a stall in each cathedral. Next must come a deanery, and then an archdeaconry, and then "peradventure God will yet add unto me something more."

The "something more" was of course a bishopric, and Nigellus proceeds to describe the methods by which such of these high offices were reached as had not been already assigned to favorites. The prelates expectant hung about the court, making presents, giving dinners, or offering their services for difficult foreign embassies. Their friends meanwhile were on the watch for sees likely to be vacant, and inquiring into their values. The age and health of the present occupants were diligently watched; the state of their teeth, their eyes, their stomachs, and reported disorders. If the accounts were conflicting, the aspirant would go himself to the spot under pretence of a pilgrimage. If the wretched bishop was found inconveniently vigorous, rumors were spread that he was shamming youth, that he was as old as Nestor, and was in his dotage; if he was infirm, it was said that men ought not to remain in positions of which they could not discharge the duties; they should go into a cloister. The king and the primate should see to it.

If intrigue failed, another road was tried. The man of the world became a saint. He retired to one or other of his churches. He was weary of the earth and its vanities, and desired to spend his remaining days in meditating upon heaven. The court dress was laid aside. The wolf clothed himself in a sheepskin, and the talk was only of prayers and ostentatious charities. · Beggars were fed in the streets, the naked were clothed, the sick were visited, the dead were buried. The rosy face grew pale, the plump cheeks became thin, and the admiring public exclaimed, " Who was like unto this man to keep the law of the Most High ? " Finally some religious order was entered in such a manner that it should be heard of everywhere. Vows were taken with an affectation of special austerities. The worthy person (who cannot see and hear him ?) would then bewail the desolations of the Church, speak in a low sad voice, sigh, walk slowly, and droop his eyelids; kings were charged with tyranny, and priests with incontinency, and all this that it might be spoken of in high places, that, when a see was vacant at last, it might be said to him, " Friend, go up higher; 'he that humbleth himself shall be exalted.' "

"Such," said Nigellus, " are the steps in our days by which men go up into the house of the Lord." By one or other of these courses success was at last attained; the recommendation of the Crown was secured, and the nomination was sent to the chapter. But the *congé d'élire* was not yet peremptory. The forms of liberty still retained some shadow of life in them, and fresh efforts were required to obtain the consent of the electors. The religious orders were the persons used on these occasions to produce the required effect; and flights of Templars, Cistercians, Carthusians, hurried to the Cathedral city to persuade the canons that the pastor whom they had never seen or never heard of, except by rumor, had more virtues than existed together in any other human being. Nigellus humorously describes the language in which these spiritual jackals portrayed their patron's merits.

He is a John the Baptist for sanctity, a Cato for wisdom, a Tully for eloquence, a Moses for meekness, a Phineas for zeal, an Abraham for faith. Elect him only, and he is all that you can desire. You ask what he has done to recommend him. Granted that he has done nothing, God can raise sons to Abraham out of the stones. He is a boy, you say, and too young for such an office; Daniel was a boy when he saved Susannah from the elders. He is of low birth; you are choosing a successor to a fisherman, not an heir to Cæsar. He is a dwarf; Jeremiah was not large. He is illiterate; Peter and Andrew were not philosophers when they were called to be apostles. He can speak no English; Augustine could speak no English, yet Augustine converted Britain. He is married and has a wife; the apostles ordered such to be promoted. He has divorced his wife; Christ separated St. John from his bride. He is immoral; so was St. Boniface. He is a fool; God has chosen the foolish things of this world to confound the wise. He is a coward; St. Joseph was a coward. He is a glutton and a wine-bibber; so Christ was said to be. He is a sluggard; St. Peter could not remain for an hour awake. He is a striker; Peter struck Malchus. He is quarrelsome; Paul quarreled with Barnabas. He is disobedient to his superiors; Paul withstood Peter. He is a man of blood; Moses killed the Egyptian. He is blind; so was Paul before he was converted. He is dumb; Zacharias was dumb. He is all faults, and possesses not a single virtue; God will make his grace so much more to abound in him.

Such eloquence and such advocates were generally irresistible. If, as sometimes happened, the Crown had named a person exceptionally infamous, or if the chapter was exceptionally obdurate, other measures lay behind. Government officers would come down and talk of enemies to the commonwealth. A bishop of an adjoining see would hint

at excommunication. The canons were worked on sep-
arately, bribed, coaxed, or threatened. The younger of
them were promised the places of the seniors. The seniors
were promised fresh offices for themselves, and promotion
for their relations. If there were two candidates and two
parties, both sides bribed, and the longest purse gained the
day. Finally the field was won. Decent members of the
chapter sighed over the disgrace, but reflected that miracles
could not be looked for.[1] The see could not remain vacant
till a saint could be found to fill it. They gave their voices
as desired. The choice was declared, the bells rang, the
organ pealed, and the choir chanted *Te Deum.*

The one touch necessary to complete the farce was then
added : —

The bishop elect, all in tears for joy, exclaims, " Depart from
me, for I am a sinful man. Depart from me, for I am unworthy.
I cannot bear the burden which you lay upon me. Alas for
my calamity! Let me alone, my beloved brethren — let me
alone in my humble state. You know not what you do." . . . .
He falls back and affects to swoon. He is borne to the archbishop to be consecrated. Other bishops are summoned to
assist, and all is finished.[2]

The scene now changed. The object was gained, the
mask was dropped, and the bishop, having reached the goal
of his ambition, could afford to show himself in his true
colors.

He has bound himself (goes on Nigellus) to be a teacher of
his flock. How can he teach those whom he sees but once a
year, and not a hundredth part of whom he even sees at all?
If any one in the diocese wants the bishop, he is told the bishop
is at court on affairs of state. He hears a hasty mass once a

---

[1] "Non sunt hæc miraculorum tempora."
[2] Now and then it happened that bishops refused to attend on these
occasions, when the person to be consecrated was notoriously infamous.
Nigellus says that one bishop at least declined to assist at the consecra-
tion of Roger, Archbishop of York.

day, *non sine tædio* (not without being bored). The rest of his time he gives to business or pleasure, and is not **b**ored. The rich get justice from him; the poor get no justice. If his metropolitan interferes with him, he appeals to Rome, and Rome protects him if he is willing to pay for it. At Rome the abbot buys his freedom from the control of the bishop; the bishop buys his freedom from the control of the archbishop. The bishop dresses as the knights dress. When his cap is on you cannot distinguish him at council from a peer. The layman swears, the bishop swears, and the bishop swears the hardest. The layman hunts, the bishop hunts. The layman hawks, the bishop hawks. Bishop and layman sit side by side at council and Treasury boards. Bishop and layman ride side by side into battle.[1] What will not bishops do? Was ever crime more atrocious than that which was lately committed in the church at Coventry?[2] When did pagan ever deal with Christian as the bishop did with the monks? I, Nigellus, saw with my own eyes, after the monks were ejected, harlots openly introduced into the cloister and chapter house to lie all night there, as in a brothel, with their paramours.[8] Such are the works of bishops in these days of ours. This is what they do, or permit to be done; and so cheap has grown the dignity of the ecclesiastical order that you will easier find a cowherd well educated than a presbyter, and an industrious duck than a literate parson.

So far Nigellus. We are not to suppose that the state of the Church had changed unfavorably in the twenty years

1 Even in the discharge of their special functions the spiritual character was scarcely more apparent. When they went on visitation, and children were brought to them to be confirmed, they gave a general blessing and did not so much as alight from their horses. Becket was the only prelate who observed common decency on these occasions. "Non enim erat ei ut plerisque, immo ut fere omnibus episcopis moris est, ministerium confirmationis equo insidendo peragere, sed ob sacramenti venerationem equo desilire et stando pueris manum imponere." — *Materials for the History of Thomas Becket*, vol. ii. p. 164.

2 In the year 1191, Hugh, Bishop of Coventry, violently expelled the monks from the cathedral there, and instituted canons in their places.

8 "Testis mihi Deus est quod dolens et tristis admodum refero quod in ecclesiâ Coventrensi oculis propriis aspexi. In claustro et capitulo vidi ego et alii nonnulli ejectis monachis meretrices publice introductas et totâ nocte cum lenonibus decubare sicut in lupanari."

which followed Becket's martyrdom, or we should have to
conclude that the spiritual enthusiasm which the martyrdom
undoubtedly excited had injured, and not improved, public
morality.

The prelates and clergy with whom Henry the Second
contended, if different at all from those of the next generation, must have been rather worse than better, and we cease
to be surprised at the language in which the king spoke of
them at Montmiraux.

Speaking generally, at the time when Becket declared
war against the State, the Church, from the Vatican to the
smallest archdeaconry, was saturated with venality. The
bishops were mere men of the world. The Church benefices were publicly bought and sold, given away as a provi-
sion to children, or held in indefinite numbers by ambitious
men who cared only for wealth and power. The mass of
the common clergy were ignorant, dissolute, and lawless,
unable to be legally married, and living with concubines in
contempt or evasion of their own rules. In character and
conduct the laity were superior to the clergy. They had
wives, and were therefore less profligate. They made no
pretensions to mysterious power and responsibilities, and
therefore they were not hypocrites. They were violent,
they were vicious, yet they had the kind of belief in the
truth of religion which bound the rope about young Henry's
neck and dragged him from his bed to die upon the ashes,
which sent them in tens of thousands to perish on the Syr-
ian sands to recover the sepulchre of Christ from the infidel. The life beyond the grave was as assured to them as
the life upon earth. In the sacraments and in the priest's
absolution lay the one hope of escaping eternal destruction.
And while they could feel no respect for the clergy as men,
they feared their powers and reverenced their office. Both
of laity and clergy the religion was a superstition, but in the
laity the superstition was combined with reverence, and
implied a real belief in the divine authority which it sym-

bolized. The clergy, the supposed depositaries of the supernatural qualities assigned to them, found it probably more difficult to believe in themselves, and the unreality revenged itself upon their natures.

Bearing in mind these qualities in the two orders, we proceed to the history of Becket.

CHAPTER II.

THOMAS BECKET was born in London in the year 1118.[1] His father, Gilbert Becket, was a citizen in moderate circumstances.[2] His name denotes Saxon extraction. Few Normans as yet were to be found in the English towns condescending to trade. Of his mother nothing authentic is known,[3] except that she was a religious woman who brought up her children in the fear of God. Many anecdotes are related of his early years, but the atmosphere of legend in which his history was so early enveloped renders them all suspicious. His parents, at any rate, both died when he was still very young, leaving him, ill provided for, to the care of his father's friends. One of them, a man of wealth, Richard de l'Aigle, took charge of the tall, handsome, clever lad. He was sent to school at Merton Abbey, in Surrey, and afterwards to Oxford. In his vacations he was thrown among young men of rank and fortune, hunting and hawking with them, cultivating his mind with the ease of conscious ability, and doubtless not inattentive to the events which were going on around him. In his nursery he must have heard of the sinking of the White Ship in the Channel with Henry the First's three children, Prince William, his brother Richard, and their sister. When he was seven years old, he may have listened to the jests of the citizens

---

1 Or 1117. The exact date is uncertain.

2 "Nec omnino infimi" are Becket's words as to the rank of his parents.

8 The story that she was a Saracen is a late legend. Becket was afterwards taunted with the lowness of his birth. The absence of any allusion to a fact so curious if it was true, either in the taunt or in Becket's reply to it, may be taken as conclusive.

at his father's table over the misadventure in London of the
cardinal legate, John of Crema. The legate had come to
England to preside at a council and pass laws to part the
clergy from their wives. While the council was going
forward, his Eminence was himself detected *in re meretriciâ*,
to general astonishment and scandal. In the same year the
Emperor Henry died. His widow, the English Matilda,
came home, and was married again soon after to Geoffrey
of Anjou. In 1134 the English barons swore fealty to her
and her young son, afterwards King Henry the Second.
The year following her father died. Her cousin, Stephen
of Blois, broke his oath and seized the crown, and general
distraction and civil war followed, while from beyond the
seas the Levant ships, as they came up the river, brought
news of bloody battles in Syria and slaughter of Christians
and infidels. To live in stirring times is the best education
of a youth of intellect. After spending three years in a
house of business in the city, Becket contrived to recommend himself to Theobald, Archbishop of Canterbury. The
archbishop saw his talents, sent him to Paris, and thence to
Bologna to study law, and employed him afterwards in the
most confidential negotiations. The description by Nigellus
of the generation of a bishop might have been copied line
for line from Becket's history. The question of the day was
the succession to the crown. Was Stephen's son, Eustace,
the heir? Or was Matilda's son, Henry of Anjou? Theobald was for Henry, so far as he dared to show himself.
Becket was sent secretly to Rome to move the pope. The
struggle ended with a compromise. Stephen was to reign
for his life. Henry was peaceably to follow him. The
arrangement might have been cut again by the sword. But
Eustace immediately afterwards died. In the same year
Stephen followed him, and Henry the Second became king
of England. With all these intricate negotiations the fut-
ure martyr was intimately connected, and by his remarkable
talents especially recommended himself to the new king.

No one called afterwards to an important position had better opportunities of acquainting himself with the spirit of the age, or the characters of the principal actors in it.[1] If his services were valuable, his reward was magnificent. He was not a priest, but again precisely as Nigellus describes, he was loaded with lucrative church benefices. He was Provost of Beverley, he was Archdeacon of Canterbury, he was rector of an unknown number of parishes, and had stalls in several cathedrals. It is noticeable that afterwards, in the heat of the battle in which he earned his saintship, he was so far from looking back with regret on this accumulation of preferments that he paraded them as an evidence of his early consequence.[2] A greater rise lay immediately before him. Henry the Second was twenty-two years old at his accession. At this time he was the most powerful prince in Western Europe. He was Duke of Normandy and Count of Anjou. His wife Eleanor, the divorced queen of Lewis of France, had brought with her Aquitaine and Poitou. The reigning pope, Adrian the Fourth, was an Englishman, and, to the grief and perplexity of later generations of Irishmen, gave the new king permission to add the Island of the Saints to his already vast dominions. Over Scotland the English monarchs asserted a semi-feudal sovereignty, to which Stephen, at the battle of the Standard, had given a semblance of reality. Few English princes'

---

[1] Very strange things were continually happening. In 1154 the Archbishop of York was poisoned in the Eucharist by some of his clergy. "Eodem anno Wilhelmus Eboracensis archiepiscopus, proditione clericorum suorum post perceptionem Eucharistiæ infra ablutiones liquore lethali infectus, extinctus est." (Hoveden, vol. i. p. 213.) Becket could not fail to have heard of this piece of villainy and to have made his own reflections upon it.

[2] Foliot, Bishop of London, told him that he owed his rise in life to the king. Becket replied : " Ad tempus quo me rex ministerio suo præstitit, archidiaconatus Cantuarensis, præpositura Beverlaci, plurimæ ecclesiæ, præbendæ nonnullæ, alia etiam non pauca quæ nominis mei erant possessio tunc temporis, adeo tenuem ut dicis, quantum ad ea quæ mundi sunt contradicunt me fuisse."

have commenced their career with fairer prospects than the second Henry.

The state of England itself demanded his first attention. The usurpation of Stephen had left behind it a legacy of disorder. The authority of the Crown had been shaken. The barons, secure behind the walls of their castles, limited their obedience by their inclinations. The Church, an *imperium in imperio,* however corrupt in practice, was aggressive as an institution, and was encroaching on the State with organized system. The principles asserted by Gregory the Seventh had been establishing themselves gradually for the past century, and in theory were no longer questioned. The power of the Crown, it was freely admitted, was derived from God. As little was it to be doubted that the clergy were the ministers of God in a nearer and higher sense than a layman could pretend to be, holding as they did the power of the keys, and able to punish disobedience by final exclusion from heaven. The principle was simple. The application only was intricate. The clergy, though divine as an order, were as frail in their individual aspect as common mortals, as ambitious, as worldly, as licentious, as unprincipled, as violent, as wicked, as much needing the restraint of law and the policeman as their secular brethren, perhaps needing it more. How was the law to be brought to bear on a class of persons who claimed to be superior to law? King Henry's piety was above suspicion, but he was at all points a sovereign, especially impatient of anarchy. The conduct of too many ecclesiastics, regular and secular alike, was entirely intolerable, and a natural impatience was spreading through the country, with which the king perhaps showed early symptoms of sympathizing. Archbishop Theobald, at any rate, was uneasy at the part which he might take, and thought that he needed some one at his side to guide him in salutary courses. At Theobald's instance, in the second year of Henry's reign, Becket became Chancellor of England, being then thirty-seven years old.

In his new dignity he seemed at first likely to disappoint the archbishop's expectations of him. Some of his biographers, indeed, claim as his perpetual merit that he opposed the *bestias curiæ*, or court wild beasts, as churchmen called the anticlerical party. John of Salisbury, on the other hand, describes him as a magnificent trifler, a scorner of law and the clergy, and given to scurrilous jesting at laymen's parties.[1] At any rate, except in the arbitrariness of his character, he showed no features of the Becket of Catholic tradition.

Omnipotent as Wolsey after him, he was no less magnificent in his outward bearing. His dress was gorgeous, his retinue of knights as splendid as the king's. His hospitalities were boundless. His expenditure was enormous. How the means for it were supplied is uncertain. The revenue was wholly in his hands. The king was often on the continent, and at such times the chancellor governed everything. He retained his Church benefices — the archdeaconry of Canterbury certainly, and probably the rest. Vast sums fell irregularly into Chancery from wardships and vacant sees and abbeys. All this Becket received, and never accounted for the whole of them. Whatever might be the explanation, the wealthiest peer in England did not maintain a more costly household, or appear in public with a more princely surrounding.

Of his administration his adoring and admiring biographer, the monk Grim, who was present at his martyrdom, draws a more than unfavorable picture, and even charges him with cruelty and ferocity. "The persons that he slew," says Grim, "the persons that he robbed of their property, no one can enumerate. Attended by a large company of knights, he would assail whole communities, destroy

---

[1] "Dum magnificus erat nugator in curiâ, dum legis videbatur contemptor et cleri, dum scurriles, cum potentioribus sectabatur ineptias, magnus habebatur, clarus erat et acceptus omnibus." — John of Salisbury to the Bishop of Exeter. Letters, 1166.

cities and towns, villages and farms, and, without remorse or pity, would give them to devouring flames." [1]

Such words give a new aspect to the demand afterwards made that he should answer for his proceedings as chancellor, and lend a new meaning to his unwillingness to reply. At this period the only virtue which Grim allows him to have preserved unsullied was his chastity.

In foreign politics he was meanwhile as much engaged as ever. The anomalous relations of the king with Lewis the Seventh, whose vassal he was for his continental dominions, while he was his superior in power, were breaking continually into quarrels, and sometimes into war. The anxiety of Henry, however, was always to keep the peace, if possible. In 1157 Becket was sent to Paris to negotiate an alliance between the Princess Margaret, Lewis's daughter, and Henry's eldest son. The prince was then seven years old. the little lady was three. Three years later they were actually married, two cardinals, Henry of Pisa and William of Pavia, coming as legates from the pope to be present on the august occasion. France and England had been at that time drawn together by a special danger which threatened Christendom. In 1159 Pope Adrian died. Alexander the Third was chosen to succeed him with the usual formalities, but the election was challenged by Frederic Barbarossa, who set up an antipope. The Catholic Church was split in two. Frederic invaded Italy, Alexander was driven out of Rome and took shelter in France at Sens. Henry and Lewis gave him their united support, and forgot their own quarrels in the common cause. Henry, it was universally admitted, was heartily in earnest for Pope Alexander. The pope, on his part, professed a willingness and an anxiety to be of corresponding service to Henry. The king

[1] "Quantis autem necem, quantis rerum omnium proscriptionem intulerit, quis enumeret? Validâ namque stipatus militum manu civitates aggressus est. Delevit urbes et oppida; villas et prædia absque miserationis intuitu voraci consumpsit incendio."— *Materials for the History of Thomas Becket,* vol. ii. pp. 364, 365.

considered the moment a favorable one for taking in hand the reform of the clergy, not as against the Holy See, but with the Holy See in active coöperation with him. On this side he anticipated no difficulty if he could find a proper instrument at home, and that instrument he considered himself to possess in his chancellor. Where the problem was to reconcile the rights of the clergy with the law of the land, it would be convenient, even essential, that the chancellorship and the primacy should be combined in the same person. Barbarossa was finding the value of such a combination in Germany, where, with the Archbishop of Cologne for a chancellor of the Empire, he was carrying out an ecclesiastical revolution.

It is not conceivable that on a subject of such vast importance the king should have never taken the trouble to ascertain Becket's views. The condition of the clergy was a pressing and practical perplexity. Becket was his confidential minister, the one person whose advice he most sought in any difficulty, and on whose judgment he most relied. Becket, in all probability, must have led the king to believe that he agreed with him. There can be no doubt whatever that he must have allowed the king to form his plans without having advised him against them, and without having cautioned him that from himself there was to be looked for nothing but opposition. The king, in fact, expected no opposition. So far as he had known Becket hitherto, he had known him as a statesman and a man of the world. If Becket had ever in this capacity expressed views unfavorable to the king's intentions, he would not have failed to remind him of it in their subsequent controversy. That he was unable to appeal for such a purpose to the king's recollection must be taken as a proof that he never did express unfavorable views. If we are not to suppose that he was deliberately insincere, we may believe that he changed his opinion in consequence of the German schism. But even so an honorable man would have given

his master warning of the alteration, and it is certain that
he did not. He did, we are told, feel some scruples. The
ecclesiastical conscience had not wholly destroyed the human conscience, and the king had been a generous master
to him. But his difficulties were set aside by the casuistries
of a Roman legate. Archbishop Theobald died when the
two cardinals were in Normandy for the marriage of Prince
Henry and the Princess Margaret. There was a year of
delay before the choice was finally made. Becket asked
the advice of Cardinal Henry of Pisa. Cardinal Henry
told him that it was for the interest of the Church that he
should accept the archbishopric, and that he need not communicate convictions which would interfere with his ap-
pointment. They probably both felt that, if Becket declined, the king would find some other prelate who would
be more pliant in his hands. Thus at last the decision was
arrived at. The Empress Matilda warned her son against
Becket's dangerous character, but the warning was in vain.
The king pressed the archbishopric on Becket, and Becket
accepted it. The Chief Justice Richard de Luci went over
with three bishops to Canterbury in the spring of 1162 to
gain the consent of the chapter; the chapter yielded not
without reluctance. The clergy of the province gave their
acquiescence at a council held afterwards at Westminster,
but with astonishment, misgiving, and secret complaints.
Becket at this time was not even a priest, and was known
only to the world as an unscrupulous and tyrannical minister. The consent was given, however. The thing was
done. On the 2d of June (1162) Becket received his
priest's orders from the Bishop of Rochester. On the 3d
he was consecrated in his own cathedral.

CHAPTER III.

BECKET was now forty-four years old. The king was thirty. The ascendency which Becket had hitherto exercised over his sovereign through the advantage of age was necessarily diminishing as the king came to maturity, and the two great antagonists, as they were henceforth to be, were more fairly matched than Becket perhaps expected to find them. The archbishop was past the time of life at which the character can be seriously changed. After forty men may alter their opinions, their policy, and their conduct; but they rarely alter their dispositions; and Becket remained as violent, as overbearing, as ambitious, as unscrupulous, as he had shown himself when chancellor, though the objects at which he was henceforth to aim were entirely different. It would be well for his memory were it possible to credit him with a desire to reform the Church of which he was the head, to purge away the corruption of it, to punish himself the moral disorders of the clergy, while he denied the right to punish them to the State. We seek in vain, however, for the slighest symptoms of any such desire. Throughout his letters there is not the faintest consciousness that anything was amiss. He had been himself amongst the grossest of pluralists; so far from being ashamed of it, he still aimed at retaining the most lucrative of his benefices. The idea with which his mind was filled was not the purity of the Church, but the privilege and supremacy of the Church. As chancellor he had been at the head of the State under the king. As archbishop, in the name of the Church, he intended to be head both of State and king; to place the pope, and himself as the pope's legate, in the position of God's vicegerents. When he found it written that "by me kings reign and princes decree judgment," he appropriated the language to himself, and his single aim was to convert the words thus construed into reality.

The first public intimation which Becket gave of his intentions was his resignation of the chancellorship. He had been made archbishop that the offices might be combined; he was no sooner consecrated than he informed the king that the duties of his sacred calling left him no leisure for secular business. He did not even wait for Henry's return from Normandy. He placed the great seal in the hands of the chief justice, the young prince, and the barons of the Exchequer, demanding and receiving from them a hurried discharge of his responsibilities. The accounts, for all that appears, were never examined. Grim, perhaps, when accusing him of rapine and murder, was referring to a suppression of a disturbance in Aquitaine, not to any special act of which he was guilty in England; but the unsparing ruthlessness which he displayed on that occasion was an indication of the disposition which was displayed in all that he did, and he was wise in anticipating inquiry.

The king had not recovered from his surprise at such unwelcome news when he learned that his splendid minister had laid aside his magnificence and had assumed the habit of a monk, that he was always in tears — tears which flowed from him with such miraculous abundance as to evidence the working in him of some special grace,[1] or else of some special purpose. His general conduct at Canterbury was equally startling. One act of charity, indeed, he had overlooked which neither in conscience nor prudence should have been forgotten. The mother of Pope Adrian the Fourth was living somewhere in his province in extreme

---

[1] "Ut putaretur possessor irrigui superioris et inferioris." The "superior" fountain of tears was the love of God; the "inferior" was the fear of hell.

poverty, starving, it was said, of cold and hunger. The see of Canterbury, as well as England, owed much to Pope Adrian, and Becket's neglect of a person who was at least entitled to honorable maintenance was not unobserved at Rome. Otherwise his generosity was profuse. Archbishop Theobald had doubled the charities of his predecessor, Becket doubled Theobald's. Mendicants swarmed about the gates of the palace; thirteen of them were taken in daily to have their dinners, to have their feet washed by the archiepiscopal hands, and to be dismissed each with a silver penny in his pocket. The tears and the benevolent humiliations were familiar in aspirants after high church offices; but Becket had nothing more to gain. What could be the meaning of so sudden and so startling a transformation? Was it penitence for his crimes as chancellor? The tears looked like penitence; but there were other symptoms of a more aggressive kind. He was no sooner in his seat than he demanded the restoration of estates that his predecessors had alienated. He gave judgment in his own court in his own favor, and enforced his own decrees. Knights holding their lands from the Church on military tenure had hitherto done homage for them to the Crown. The new archbishop demanded the homage for himself. He required the Earl of Clare to swear fealty to him for Tunbridge Castle. The Earl of Clare refused and appealed to the king, and the archbishop dared not at once strike so large a quarry. But he showed his teeth with a smaller offender. Sir William Eynesford, one of the king's knights, was patron of a benefice in Kent. The archbishop presented a priest to it. The knight ejected the archbishop's nominee, and the archbishop excommunicated the knight. Such peremptory sentences, pronounced without notice, had a special inconvenience when directed against persons immediately about the king. Excommunication was like the plague; whoever came near the infected body himself caught the contagion, and the king might be poisoned without his knowledge. It had been usual in these cases to pay the king the courtesy of consulting him. Becket, least of all men, could have pleaded ignorance of such a custom. It seemed that he did not choose to observe it.[1] While courting the populace, and gaining a reputation as a saint among the clergy, the archbishop was asserting his secular authority, and using the spiritual sword to enforce it. Again, what did it mean, this interference with the rights of the laity, this ambition for a personal following of armed knights? Becket was not a dreamer who had emerged into high place from the cloister or the library. He was a man of the world intimately acquainted with the practical problems of the day, the most unlikely of all persons to have adopted a course so marked without some ulterior purpose. Henry discovered too late that his mother's eyes had been keener than his own. He returned to England in the beginning of 1163. Becket met him at his landing, but was coldly received.

In the summer of the same year, Pope Alexander held a council at Tours. The English prelates attended. The question of precedence was not this time raised. The Archbishop of Canterbury and his suffragans sat on the pope's right hand, the Archbishop of York and his suffragans sat on the pope's left. Whether anything of consequence passed on this occasion between the pope and Becket is not known: probably not; it is certain, however, that they met. On the archbishop's return to England the disputes between the secular and spiritual authorities broke into open conflict.

The Church principles of Gregory the Seventh were

---

[1] " Quod, quia rege minime certiorato archiepiscopus fecisset, maximam ejus indignationem incurrit. Asserit enim rex juxta dignitatem regni sui, quod nullus qui de rege teneat in capite vel minister ejus citra ipsius conscientiam sit excommunicandus ab aliquo, ne si hoc regem lateat lapsus ignorantiâ communicet excommunicato ; comitem vel baronem ad se venientem in osculo vel consilio admittat." — Matthew Paris, *Chronica Majora*, vol. ii. p. 222.

making their way through Europe, but were making their way with extreme slowness. Though the celibacy of the clergy had been decreed by law, clerical concubinage was still the rule in England. A *focaria* and a family were still to be found in most country parsonages. In theory the priesthood was a caste. In practice priests and their flocks were united by common interests, common pursuits, common virtues, and common crimes. The common law of England during the reigns of the Conqueror's sons had refused to distinguish between them. Clerks guilty of robbery or murder had been tried like other felons in the ordinary courts, and if found guilty had suffered the same punishments. The new pretension was that they were a peculiar order, set apart for God's service, not amenable to secular jurisdiction, and liable to trial only in the spiritual courts. Under the loose administration of Stephen the judges had begun to recognize their immunity, and the conduct of the lower class of clergy was in consequence growing daily more intolerable. Clergy, indeed, a great many of them had no title to be called. They had received only some minor form of orders, of which no sign was visible in their appearance or conduct. They were clerks only so far as they held benefices and claimed special privileges; for the rest, they hunted, fought, drank, and gambled like other idle gentlemen.

In the autumn of 1163 a specially gross case of clerical offence brought the question to a crisis.

Philip de Broi, a young nobleman who held a canonry at Bedford, had killed some one in a quarrel. He was brought before the court of the Bishop of Lincoln, where he made his purgation *ecclesiastico jure* — that is to say, he paid the usual fees and perhaps a small fine. The relations of the dead man declared themselves satisfied, and Philip de Broi was acquitted. The Church and the relations might be satisfied; public justice was not satisfied. The sheriff of Bedfordshire declined to recognize the decision, and summoned the canon a second time. The canon insulted the sheriff in open court, and refused to plead before him. The sheriff referred the matter to the king. The king sent for Philip de Broi, and cross-questioned him in Becket's presence. It was not denied that he had killed a man. The king inquired what Becket was prepared to do. Becket's answer, for the present and all similar cases, was that a clerk in orders accused of felony must be tried in the first instance in an ecclesiastical court, and punished according to ecclesiastical law. If the crime was found to be of peculiarly dark kind, the accused might be deprived of his orders, and, if he again offended, should lose his privilege. But for the offence for which he was deprived be was not to be again tried or again punished; the deprivation itself was to suffice.

The king, always moderate, was unwilling to press the question to extremity. He condemned the judgment of the Bishop of Lincoln's court. He insisted that the murderer should have a real trial. But he appointed a mixed commission of bishops and laymen to try him, the bishops having the preponderating voice.

Philip de Broi pleaded that he had made his purgation in the regular manner, that he had made his peace with the family of the man that he had killed, and that the matter was thus ended. He apologized for having insulted the sheriff, and professed himself willing to make reasonable reparation. The sentence of the commission was that his benefices should be sequestered for two years, and that, if the sheriff insisted upon it, he should be flogged.

So weak a judgment showed Henry the real value of Becket's theory. The criminal clerk was to be amenable to the law as soon as he has been degraded, not before; and it was perfectly plain, that clerks never would be degraded. They might commit murder upon murder, robbery upon robbery, and the law would be unable to touch them. It could not be. The king insisted that a sacred profession

should not be used as a screen for the protection of felony.
He summoned the whole body of the bishops to meet him
in a council at Westminster in October.

The council met.   The archbishop was resolute.   He
replied for the other bishops in an absolute refusal to make
any concession.   The judges and the laity generally were
growing excited.   Had the clergy been saints, the claims
advanced for them would have been scarcely tolerable.
Being what they were, such pretensions were ridiculous.
Becket might speak in their name.   He did not speak their
real opinions.   Arnulf, Bishop of Lisieux, came over to use
his influence with Becket, but he found him inexorable.   To
risk the peace of the Church in so indefensible a quarrel
seemed obstinate folly.   The Bishop of Lisieux and several
of the English prelates wrote privately to the pope to entreat him to interfere.

Alexander had no liking for Becket.   He had known
him long, and had no belief in the lately assumed airs of
sanctity.   Threatened as he was by the emperor and the
antipope, he had no disposition to quarrel with Henry, nor
in the particular question at issue does he seem to have
thought the archbishop in the right.   On the spot he dispatched a legate, a monk named Philip of Aumone, to tell
Becket that he must obey the laws of the realm, and submit
to the king's pleasure.

The king was at Woodstock.   The archbishop, thus commanded, could not refuse to obey.   He repaired to the
court.   He gave his promise.   He undertook, *bonâ fide et
sine malo ingenio*, to submit to the laws of the land, whatever they might be found to be.   But a vague engagement
of this kind was unsatisfactory, and might afterwards be
evaded.   The question of the immunities of the clergy had
been publicly raised.   The attention of the nation had been
called to it.   Once for all the position in which the clergy
were to stand to the law of the land must be clearly and
finally laid down.   The judges had been directed to inquire

into the customs which had been of use in England under the king's grandfather, Henry the First. A second council was called to meet at Clarendon, near Winchester, in the following January, when these customs, reduced to writing, would be placed in the archbishops' and bishops' hands, and they would be required to consent to them in detail.

The spiritual power had encroached on many sides. Every question, either of person, conduct, or property, in which an ecclesiastic was a party, the Church courts had endeavored to reserve for themselves. Being judges in their own causes, the decisions of the clergy were more satisfactory to themselves than to the laity. The practice of appealing to Rome in every cause in which a churchman was in any way connected had disorganized the whole course of justice. The Constitutions (as they were called) of Clarendon touched in detail on a variety of points on which the laity considered themselves injured. The general provisions embodied in these famous resolutions would now be scarcely challenged in the most Catholic country in the world.

1. During the vacancy of any archbishopric, bishopric, abbey, or priory of royal foundation, the estates were to be in the custody of the Crown. Elections to these preferments were to be held in the royal chapel, with the assent of the king and council.

2. In every suit to which a clerk was a party, proceedings were to commence before the king's justices, and these justices were to decide whether the case was to be tried before a spiritual or a civil court. If it was referred to a spiritual court, a civil officer was to attend to watch the trial, and if a clerk was found guilty of felony the Church was to cease to protect him.

3. No tenant-in-chief of the king, or officer of his household, was to be excommunicated, or his lands laid under an interdict, until application had been first made to the king, or, in his absence, to the chief justice.

4. Laymen were not to be indicted in a bishop's court, either for perjury or other similar offence, except in the bishop's presence by a lawful prosecutor and with lawful witnesses. If the accused was of so high rank that no prosecutor would appear, the bishop might require the sheriff to call a jury to inquire into the case.

5. Archbishops, bishops, and other great persons were forbidden to leave the realm without the king's permission.

6. Appeals were to be from the archdeacon to the bishop, from the bishop to the archbishop, from the archbishop to the king, and no further; that, by the king's mandate, the case might be ended in the archbishop's court.[1]

The last article the king afterwards explained away. It was one of the most essential, but he was unable to maintain it; and he was rash, or he was ill-advised, in raising a second question, on which the pope would naturally be sensitive, before he had disposed of the first. On the original subject of dispute, whether benefit of clergy was to mean impunity to crime, the pope had already practically decided, and he could have been brought without difficulty to give a satisfactory judgment upon it. Some limit also might have been assigned to the powers of excommunication which could be so easily abused, and which, if abused, might lose their terrors. But appeals to the pope were the most lucrative source of the pope's revenue. To restrict appeals was to touch at once his pride and his exchequer.

The Constitutions were drafted, and when the council assembled were submitted to Becket for approval. He saw in the article on the appeals a prospect of recovering Alexander's support, and he again became obstinate. None of the bishops, however, would stand by him. There was a general entreaty that he would not reopen the quarrel, and he yielded so far as to give a general promise of conform-

---

[1] The Constitutions were seventeen in all. The articles in the text are an epitome of those which the Church found most objectionable.

ity.[1] It was a promise given dishonestly — given with a conscious intention of not observing it. He had been tempted, he afterwards said, by an intimation that, if he would but seem to yield, the king would be satisfied, Becket was a lawyer. He could not really have been under any such illusion. In real truth he did not mean to be bound by the language of the Constitutions at all, but only by his own language, from which it would be easy to escape. The king by this time knew the man with whom he had to deal. The Constitutions were placed in writing before the bishops, who one and all were required to signify their adherence under their several hands and seals.

Becket, we are innocently told by his biographer Grim, now saw that he was to be entrapped. There was no entrapping if his promise had been honestly given. The use of the word is a frank confession that he had meant to deceive Henry by words, and that he was being caught in his own snare. When driven to bay, the archbishop's fiery nature always broke into violence. "Never, never," he said; "I will never do it so long as breath is in my body."[2] In affected penitence for his guilty compliance, he retired to his see to afflict his flesh with public austerities. He suspended himself *ab altaris officio* (from the service of the altar) till the pope should absolve him from his sin. The Bishop of Evreux, who was present at Clarendon, advised him to write to the pope for authority to sign. He pretended to comply, but he commissioned a private friend of

---

[1] Foliot, however, says that many of the bishops were willing to stand out, and that Becket himself advised a false submission (Foliot to Becket, Giles, vol. i. p. 381.)

[2] Sanctus archiepiscopus tunc primum dolum quem fuerat suspicatus advertens, interpositâ fide quam Deo debuit: "Non hoc fiet," respondit, "quam diu in hoc vasculo spirat hæc anima." Nam domestici regis securum fecerant archiepiscopum quod nunquam scriberentur leges, nunquam illarum fieret recordatio, si regem verbo tantum in audientiâ procerum honorasset. Fictâ se conjuratione seductum videns, ad animam usque tristabatur." — *Materials for the History of Thomas Becket*, vol. ii. p. 382.

his own, John of Salisbury, who was on the continent, to prepare for his reception on the flight which he already meditated from England, and by all methods, fair and foul, to prevent the pope and cardinals from giving the king any further encouragement. The Bishop of Lisieux, on the other hand, whose previous intercession had decided the pope in the king's favor, went to Sens in person to persuade Alexander to cut the knot by sending legatine powers to the Archbishop of York, to override Becket's obstinacy and to consent in the name of the Church instead of him.

John of Salisbury's account of his proceedings gives a curious picture of the cause of God, as Becket called it, on its earthly and grosser side.

The Count of Flanders (he wrote to the archbishop) is most anxious to help you. If extremity comes, send the count word, and he will provide ships.[1] Everything which passed in London and at Winchester (Clarendon) is better known here than in England itself. I have seen the King of France, who undertakes to write to the pope in your behalf. The feeling towards our king among the French people is of fear and hatred. The pope himself I have avoided so far. I have written to the two cardinals of Pisa and Pavia to explain the injury which will ensue to the Court of Rome if the Constitutions are upheld. I am not sanguine, however. "Many things make against us, few in our favor. Great men will come over here with money to spend, *quam nunquam Roma contempsit* (which Rome never despised). The pope himself has always been against us in this cause, and throws in our teeth that after all which Pope Adrian did for the see of Canterbury you are allowing his mother to starve in cold and hunger."[2] You write that if I cannot succeed otherwise I may promise two hundred marks. The other side will give down three or four hundred sooner than be defeated,[3] and I will answer for the Romans that

---

[1] "Naves enim procurabit si hoc necessitas vestra exegerit, et ipse ante, ut oportet, præmoneatur." — *Joannis Sarisbiriensis Epistolæ*, vol. i. p. 189.

[2] "Cujus mater apud vos algore torquetur et inediâ."

[3] "Sed scribitis, si alia via non patuerit, promittamus ducentas marcas. At certe pars adversa antequam frustretur trecentas dabit aut quadringentas."

they will prefer the larger sum in hand from the king to the smaller in promise from you. It is true we are contending for the liberties of the Church, but your motive, it will be said, is not the Church's welfare, but your own ambition. They will propose (I have already heard a whisper of it) that the pope shall cross to England in person to crown the young king and take your place at Canterbury for a while. If the Bishop of Lisieux sees the pope, he will do mischief. I know the nature of him.[1]

Though the archbishop was convulsing the realm for the sacred right of appeals to Rome, it is plain from this letter that he was aware of the motives by which the papal decisions were governed, and that he was perfectly ready to address himself to them. Unfortunately his resources were limited, and John of Salisbury's misgivings were confirmed. The extraordinary legatine powers were conceded not to the Archbishop of York — it was held inexpedient to set York above Canterbury — but to the king himself. To Becket the pope wrote with some irony on hearing that he had suspended himself. He trusted the archbishop was not creating needless scandal. The promise to the king had been given with good intentions, and could not therefore be a serious sin. If there was anything further on his conscience (did the pope suspect that the promise had been dishonest?), he might confess it to any discreet priest. He (the pope) meanwhile absolved him, and advised, and even enjoined, him to return to his duties.

The first campaign was thus over, and the king was so far victorious. The legatine powers having arrived, the Constitutions were immediately acted upon. The number of criminals among the clergy happened to be unusually large.[2] They were degraded, sent to trial, and suffered in the usual way by death or mutilation. "Then," say Beck-

---

[1] John of Salisbury to Becket (abridged). Letters, vol. i. p. 187.

[2] "Sed et ordinatorum inordinati mores inter regem et archiepiscopum auxere malitiam, qui solito abundantius per idem tempus apparebant, publicis irretiti criminibus." — *Materials*, etc., vol. ii. p. 385.

et's despairing biographers, " was seen the mournful spectacle of priests and deacons who had committed murder, manslaughter, theft, robbery, and other crimes, carried in carts before the king's commissioners, and punished as if they had been ordinary men." The archbishop clamored, threatened, and, as far as his power went, interfered. The king was firm. He had sworn at his coronation, he said, to do justice in the realm, and there were no greater villains in it than many of the clergy.[1] That bishops should take public offenders out of custody, absolve them, and let them go, was not to be borne. It was against law, against usage, against reason. It could not be. The laity were generally of the king's opinion. Of the bishops some four or five agreed privately with Becket, but dared not avow their opinions. The archbishop perceived that the game was lost unless he could himself see the pope and speak to him. He attempted to steal over from Sandwich, but the boatmen recognized him midway across the channel and brought him back.

[1] " In omni scelere et flagitio nequiores."

CHAPTER IV.

THE pope had sent legatine powers to the king, and the king had acted upon them; but something was still wanting for general satisfaction. He had been required to confirm the Constitutions by a bull. He had hesitated to do it, and put off his answer. At length he sent the Archbishop of Rouen to England to endeavor to compromise matters. The formal consent of the Church was still wanting, and in the absence of it persons who agreed with the king in principle were uneasy at the possible consequences. The clergy might be wicked, but they were magicians notwithstanding, and only the chief magician could make it safe to deal with them. In the autumn of 1164 the king once more summoned a great council to meet him at Northampton Castle. The attendance was vast. Every peer and prelate not disabled was present, all feeling the greatness of the occasion. Castle, town, and monasteries were thronged to overflowing. Becket only had hesitated to appear. His attempt to escape to the continent was constructive treason. It was more than treason. It was a violation of a distinct promise which he had given to the king.[1] The storm which he had raised had unloosed the tongues of those who had to complain of his ill-usage of them either in his archbishop's court or in the days when he was chancellor. The accounts had been looked into, and vast sums were found to have been received by him of which no explanation had been given. Who was this man, that he should throw the country into confusion, in the teeth of the bishops, in the teeth (as it seemed) of the pope, in the teeth of his own oath

---

[1] Foliot to Becket, Giles, vol. ii. p. 387.

given solemnly to the king at Woodstock? The Bishop of
London, in a letter to Becket, charged him with having
directly intended to commit perjury.[1] The first object of
the Northampton council was to inquire into his conduct,
and he had good reason to be alarmed at the probable consequences. He dared not, however, disobey a peremptory
summons. He came, attended by a large force of armed
knights, and was entertained at the monastery of St. An-
drews. To anticipate inquiry into his attempted flight, he
applied for permission on the day of his arrival to go to
France to visit the pope. The king told him that he could
not leave the realm until he had answered for a decree which
had been given in his court. The case was referred to the
assembled peers, and he was condemned and fined. It was
a bad augury for him. Other charges lay thick, ready to
be produced. He was informed officially that he would be
required to explain the Chancery accounts, and answer for
the money which he had applied to his own purposes. His
proud temper was chafed to the quick, and he turned sick
with anger.[2] His admirers see only in these demands the
sinister action of a dishonest tyranny. Oblique accusations,
it is said, were raised against him, either to make him bend
or to destroy his character. The question is rather whether
his conduct admitted of explanation. If he had been unjust as a judge, if he had been unscrupulous as a high officer of state, such faults had no unimportant bearing on his
present attitude. He would have done wisely to clear himself if he could; it is probable that he could not. He refused to answer, and he sheltered himself behind the release
which he had received at his election. His refusal was not
allowed; a second summons the next day found him in his

[1] Foliot says that at Clarendon Becket said to the bishops, "It is the
Lord's will I should perjure myself. For the present I submit and incur
perjury, to repent of it, however, as I best may." — Giles, vol. i. p. 381.
Foliot was reminding Becket of what passed on that occasion.

[2] "Propter iram et indignationem quam in animo conceperat decidit in
gravem ægritudinem." — Hoveden, vol. i. p. 225.

bed, which he said that he was too ill to leave. This was on a Saturday. A respite was allowed him until the following Monday. On Monday the answer was the same. Messenger after messenger brought back word that the archbishop was unable to move. The excuse might be true — perhaps partially it was true. The king sent two great peers to ascertain, and in his choice of persons he gave a conclusive answer to the accusation of desiring to deal unfairly with Becket; one was Reginald, Earl of Cornwall, the king's uncle, who as long as Becket lived was the best friend that he had at the court; the other was the remarkable Robert, Earl of Leicester, named Bossu (the Hunchback). This Robert was a monk of Leicester Abbey, though he had a dispensation to remain at the court, and so bitter a papist was he that when the schismatic Archbishop of Cologne came afterwards to London he publicly insulted him and tore down the altar at which he had said mass. Such envoys would not have been selected with a sinister purpose. They found that the archbishop could attend if he wished, and they warned him of the danger of trying the king too far. He pleaded for one more day. On the Tuesday morning he undertook to be present.

His knights, whose first allegiance was to the Crown, had withdrawn from the monastery, not daring or not choosing to stand by a prelate who appeared to be defying his sovereign. Their place had been taken by a swarm of mendicants, such as the archbishop had gathered about him at Canterbury. He prepared for the scene in which he was to play a part with the art of which he was so accomplished a master. He professed to expect to be killed. He rose early. Some of the bishops came to see and remonstrate with him : they could not move his resolution, and they retired. Left to himself, he said the mass of St. Stephen in which were the words: "The kings of the earth stood up, and the rulers took counsel together against the Lord and against his anointed." He then put on a black stole and cap, mounted his palfrey, and, followed by a few monks and surrounded by his guard of beggars, rode a foot's pace to the castle preceded by his cross-bearer.

The royal castle of Northampton was a feudal palace of the usual form. A massive gateway led into a quadrangle; across the quadrangle was the entrance of the great hall, and at the upper end of the hall doors opened into spacious chambers beyond. The archbishop alighted at the gate, himself took his cross in his right hand, and, followed by a small train, passed through the quadrangle, and passed up the hall, " looking like the lion-man of the prophet's vision." [1] The king and the barons were in one chamber, the bishops in another. The archbishop was going in this attitude into the king's presence, that the court might see the person on whom they dared to sit in judgment; but certain " Templars " warned him to beware. He entered among his brethren, and moved through them to a chair at the upper end of the room.

He still held his cross. The action was unusual; the cross was the spiritual sword, and to bear it thus conspicuously in a deliberative assembly was as if a baron had entered the council in arms. The mass of St. Stephen had been heard of, and in the peculiar temper of men's minds was regarded as a magical incantation.[2] The Bishop of Hereford advanced and offered to carry the cross for him. Foliot, Bishop of London (*filius hujus sæculi*, " a son of this world ") said that if he came thus armed into the court the king would draw a sharper sword, and he would see then what his arms would avail him. Seeing him still obstinate, Foliot tried to force the cross out of his hands. The Archbishop of York added his persuasions; but the Archbishop of York peculiarly irritated Becket, and was

---

[1] "Assumens faciem hominis, faciem leonis, propheticis illis animalibus a prophetâ descriptis simillimus." — Herbert of Bosham.

[2] It was said to have been done *per artem magicam et in contemptu regis*. (Hoveden.) He had the eucharist concealed under his dress.

silenced by a violent answer. "Fool thou hast ever been," said the Bishop of London, "and from thy folly I see plainly thou wilt not depart." Cries burst out on all sides. "Fly!" some one whispered in the archbishop's ear; "fly, or you are a dead man." The Bishop of Exeter came in at the moment, and exclaimed that unless the archbishop gave way they would all be murdered. Becket never showed to more advantage than in moments of personal danger. To the Bishop of Exeter he gave a sharp answer, telling him that he savored not the things of God. But he collected himself. He saw that he was alone. He stood up, he appealed to the pope, charged the bishops on peril of their souls to excommunicate any one who dared to lay hands on him, and moved as if he intended to withdraw. The Bishop of Winchester bade him resign the archbishopric. With an elaborate oath (*cum interminabili juratione*) he swore that he would not resign. The Bishop of Chichester then said: "As our primate we are bound to obey you, but you are our primate no longer; you have broken your oath. You swore allegiance to the king, and you subvert the common law of the realm. We too appeal to the pope. To his presence we summon you." "I hear what you say," was all the answer which Becket deigned to return.

The doors from the adjoining chamber were now flung open. The old Earl of Cornwall, the hunchback Leicester, and a number of barons entered. "My lord," said the Earl of Leicester to the archbishop, "the king requires you to come to his presence and answer to certain things which will then be alleged against you, as you promised yesterday to do." "My lord earl," said Becket, "thou knowest how long and loyally I served the king in his worldly affairs. For that cause it pleased him to promote me to the office which now I hold. I did not desire the office; I knew my infirmities. When I consented it was for the sake of the king alone. When I was elected I was formally acquitted of my responsibilities for all that I had done as chancellor. Therefore I am not bound to answer, and I will not answer."

The earls carried back the reply. The peers by a swift vote declared that the archbishop must be arrested and placed under guard.

The earls reëntered, and Leicester approached him and began slowly and reluctantly to announce the sentence. " Nay," said Becket, lifting his tall meagre figure to its haughtiest height, " do thou first listen to me. The child may not judge his father. The king may not judge me, nor may you judge me. I will be judged under God by the pope alone, to whom in your presence I appeal. I forbid you under anathema to pronounce your sentence. And you, my brethren," he said, turning to the bishops, "since you will obey man rather than God, I call you too before the same judgment-seat. Under the protection of the Apostolic See, I depart hence."

No hand was raised to stop him. He swept through the chamber and flung open the door of the hall. He stumbled on the threshold, and had almost fallen, but recovered himself. The October evening was growing into twilight. The hall was thronged with the retinues of the king and the barons. Dinner was over. The floor was littered with rushes and fragments of rolls and broken meat. Draughts of ale had not been wanting, and young knights, pages, and retainers were either lounging on the benches or talking in eager and excited groups. As Becket appeared among them, fierce voices were heard crying, "Traitor! traitor! Stop the traitor!" Among the loudest were Count Hamelin, the king's illegimate brother, and Sir Ranulf de Broc, one of the Canterbury knights. Like a bold animal at bay, Becket turned sharply on these two. He called Count Hamelin a bastard boy. He reminded De Broc of some near kinsman of his who had been hanged. The cries rose into a roar; sticks and knots of straw were flung at him. Another rash word, and he might have been torn in pieces. Some high official hearing the noise came in and conducted him safely to the door.

In the quadrangle he found his servants waiting with his palfrey. The great gate was locked, but the key was hanging on the wall; one of them took it and opened the gate, the porters looking on, but not interfering. Once outside he was received with a cheer of delight from the crowd, and with a mob of people about him he made his way back to the monastery. The king had not intended to arrest him, but he could not know it, and he was undoubtedly in danger from one or other of the angry men with whom the town was crowded. He prepared for immediate flight. A bed was made for him in the chapel behind the altar. After a hasty supper with a party of beggars whom he had intro-
ced into the house, he lay down for a few hours of rest.
vo in the morning, in a storm of wind and rain, he stole
isguised with two of the brethren. He reached Lin-
after daybreak, and from Lincoln, going by cross
lipping from hiding-place to hiding-place, he
a fortnight to a farm of his own at Eastry,
He was not pursued. It was no sooner
one from Northampton than a procla-
the country forbidding every man
eddle with him. The king had
l, and once more to place the
ds. The Earl of Arundel
s dispatched at once to
and to request Alex-
stigate the quarrel
ve consented to
t Canterbury
e result ew too well
the forces which would be at work in the papal court to wait for its verdict. His confidence was only in himself. Could he see the pope in person, he thought that he could

influence him. He was sure of the friendship of Lewis of France, who was meditating a fresh quarrel with Henry, and would welcome his support. His own spiritual weapons would be as effective across the Channel as if used in England, while he would himself be in personal security. One dark night he went down with his two companions into Sandwich, and in an open boat crossed safely to Gravelines. At St. Omer he fell in with his old friend Chief Justice de Luci, who was returning from a mission to the court of France. De Luci urged him to return to England and wait for the pope's decision, warning him of the consequences of persisting in a course which was really treasonable, and undertaking that the king would forgive him if he would go back at once. Entreaties and warnings were alike thrown away. He remained and dispatched a letter to the pope saying briefly that he had followed the example of his holiness in resisting the encroachments of princes, and had fled from his country. He had been called to answer before the king as if he had been a mere layman. The bishops, who ought to have stood by him, had behaved like cowards. If he was not sustained by his holiness, the Church would be ruined, and he would himself be doubly confounded.

•

CHAPTER V.

THE king and the English bishops looked with reasonable confidence to the result of their appeal. Becket had broken his promise to accept the Constitutions, and had so broken it as to show that the promise had been given in conscious bad faith. He was a defaulting public officer. He had been unjust as a judge. He had defied the Crown and the estates of the realm. He had refused to answer for his conduct, and had denied his responsibilities. He had deserted his post, and had fled from the realm, although the king's proclamation had left him without the excuse that he was in fear of personal violence. He was an archbishop, and possessed, in virtue of his office, of mysterious powers which the laity had not learned to defy. But the pope was superior to him in his own sphere, and on the pope the king naturally felt that he had a right to rely. The Earl of Arundel with the other peers, the Archbishop of York, and the Bishops of London, Chichester, and Exeter, were chosen as envoys, and were dispatched immediately on the dissolution of the Northampton meeting. They crossed the Channel on the same night that Becket crossed, and after a hasty and unsatisfactory interview with Lewis at Compiègne they made their way to Sens. Becket ought to have met them there. But Becket preferred to feel his ground and make friends in France before presenting himself. He was disappointed in the Count of Flanders, who declined to countenance him. He escaped in disguise over the French frontier, and addressed himself to Lewis at Soissons. Lewis, who meant no good to Henry, received him warmly, and wrote in his favor to the pope. At the French court he remained till he saw how matters would go at Sens, sending forward his confidential friend, Herbert of Bosham, to watch the proceedings, and speak for him to the pope and cardinals.

He might have easily been present himself, since Herbert reached Sens only a day after the arrival of the English ambassadors. The bishops stated their case. They laid the blame of the quarrel on the archbishop's violence. They explained the moderation of the king's demands. They requested the pope's interposition. The Earl of Arundel followed in the name of the English barons. He dwelt on the fidelity with which the king had adhered to the Holy See in its troubles, and the regret with which, if justice was denied them, the English nation might be compelled to look elsewhere. He requested, and the bishops requested, that Becket should be ordered to return to Canterbury, and that a legate or legates should be sent with plenary powers to hear the cause and decide upon it.

Seeing that the question immediately before the pope did not turn on the Constitutions, but on the liability of the archbishop to answer for his civil administration, the king was making a large concession. Many cardinals had their own good reasons for being on the the king's side, and, if left to himself, the pope would have been glad to oblige a valuable friend. But to favor Henry was to offend Lewis under whose shelter he had taken refuge. The French bishops were many of them as violent as Becket himself. The French people were on the same side from natural enmity to England, and Pope Alexander was in the same difficulty in which Pope Clement found himself three centuries later between Henry the Eighth and Charles the Fifth. He said that he could form no resolution till he had heard what Becket had to say. He suggested that the English envoys should wait for Becket's arrival; but it was uncertain when Becket might arrive; his French friends were gathering in their rear, and might intercept their return. A protracted stay was impossible, and they again pressed for a legate. Alexander agreed to send some one, but without the ample powers which the envoys desired. He reserved the final decision for himself.

The influences by which the papal court was determined were already too grossly notorious. A decision given in France would be the decision which would please the King of France. The envoys went home, taking with them a complimentary nuncio from the pope, and they had some difficulty in escaping an attempt to waylay and capture them.

They had no sooner gone than Becket appeared at Sens. He was received with no great warmth by the pope, and still more coldly by the cardinals "whose nostrils the scent of lucre had infected."[1] French pressure, however, soon produced its effect. He had come magnificently attended from Soissons. His cause was openly espoused by the French nation. At his second interview, on his knees at Alexander's feet he represented that he was the victim of his devotion to the Holy See and the Catholic faith. He had only to yield on the Constitutions to be restored at once to favor and power. The Constitutions were read over, and he asked how it was possible for him to acknowledge laws which reduced the clergy into common mortals, and restricted appeals to the last depositary of justice on earth.

Herbert of Bosham states that the pope and cardinals had never yet seen the Constitutions, but had only heard of them. This is simply incredible, and, like many other stories of this interesting but interested writer, is confuted by the facts of the case. John of Salisbury had said that the proceedings at Clarendon were better known on the continent than in England. They had been watched in France for almost a year with the closest attention. Bishops and abbots had gone to and fro between the pope and the English court with no other object than to find some terms of

---

[1] "Quorum nares odor lucri infecerat."

compromise. It is not conceivable that after sending an order to Becket to submit, after Becket had first consented, had then suspended himself for the sin of acquiescence, and had been absolved by Alexander himself, the Holy Father should never have acquainted himself with the particulars of the controversy. It is no less incredible, therefore, that, after hearing the Constitutions read, the pope should have severely blamed Becket, as Herbert also says that he did, for having ever consented at all. Be this as it may, the Constitutions found no favor. Parts of them were found tolerable, but parts intolerable, especially the restriction of the appeals. Again the pope took time for reflection. English money had secured a powerful faction among his advisers, and they were not ungrateful. Henry, they said, would no doubt modify the objectionable articles; and it was unsafe to alienate him at so dangerous a time. In private they sharply blamed Becket for having raised so inopportune a storm; and but for his own adroitness the archbishop would have been defeated after all. Once more he sought the pope's presence. He confessed his sins, and he tempted Alexander with the hope of rescuing the nomination to the see of Canterbury from secular interference. He had been intruded into Christ's sheepfold, he said, by the secular power;[1] and from this source all his subsequent troubles had arisen. The bishops at Northampton had bade him resign. He could not resign at their bidding, but he threw himself and his office on his holiness's mercy. He had accepted the archbishopric uncanonically. He now relinquished it, to be restored or not restored as the pope might please.

It was a bold stroke, and it nearly failed. Many cardi-

---

[1] "Ascendi in ovile Christi, sed non per ipsum ostium: velut quem non canonica vocavit electio, sed terror publicæ potestatis intrusit." — *Materials for the History of Thomas à Becket*, vol. ii. p. 243. But all these accounts of conversations must be received with caution. The accounts vary irreconcilably; and the enthusiasm of the biographers for their master and his cause infects every line of their narrative.

nals saw in the offer a road out of the difficulty. Terms could now be arranged with Henry, and Becket could be provided for elsewhere. For some hours or days his friends thought his cause was lost. But the balance wavered at last so far in his favor that the sacrifice was not permitted. He was not, as he had expected, to be sent back in triumph to England supported by threats of interdict and excommunication to triumph over his enemies. But he was reinstated as archbishop. He was assigned a residence at the Cistercian monastery of Pontigny, thirty miles from Sens; and there he was directed to remain quiet and avoid for the present irritating the king further.[1]

The king was sufficiently irritated already. The support which Lewis had given to Becket meant too probably that war with France was not far off. Becket himself was virtually in rebellion, and his character made it easy to foresee the measures which he would adopt if not prevented. The posts were watched, strangers were searched for letters. English subjects were forbidden to introduce brief, bull, or censure either from the pope or from the archbishop. The archbishop's estates were sequestrated. Were he allowed to retain his large income and spend it abroad, he would use it to buy friends among the cardinals. The see was put under administrators — the rents, so Henry afterwards swore, were chiefly laid out in management, and the surplus was distributed in charity. The incumbents of the archbishop's benefices being his special creatures were expelled, and loyal priests were put in their places. Another harder measure was adopted. All his relations, all his connections and dependents, except a few who gave securities for good conduct, were banished from England, four hundred of them, men, women, and children. Either it was feared the

---

[1] The answer supposed to have been given by the pope, permitting him to use the censures, belongs to the following year. It refers to the sequestration of the Canterbury estates, and this did not take place till after Becket had been settled at Pontigny.

4

archbishop would employ them to disturb the country, or it was mere vengeance, or it was to make Becket an expensive guest to Lewis.

All this Becket was obliged to bear with. Armed as he was with lightnings, he was forbidden to make use of them. Nay, worse, the pope himself could not even yet be depended on. Angry as he was, the king wrote to propose that Alexander should visit him in England, or, if this were impossible, that the pope, Lewis, and Henry should meet in Normandy and take measures together for the common welfare of Christendom. Henry had no wish to join Barbarossa if he could help it; and neither the pope nor Lewis could wish to force him. If such a meeting came off, it was easy to foresee the issue. John of Salisbury, who was Becket's agent at the French court, when he heard what was intended, wrote that it must be prevented at all hazards. In terms not very complimentary to the holy father's understanding, the archbishop implored Alexander to consent to no meeting with the King of England, except one at which he should himself be present. "The king," he said, "is so subtle with his words that he would confound the apostolic religion itself. He will find the weak points of the pope's character, and will trip him up to his destruction." [1]

The King of France (John of Salisbury wrote to Becket) admits that he fears to urge the pope to use the censures in your behalf. If this be so now, how will it be when our king is here in person, arguing, promising, and threatening with the skill which you know that he possesses? He has secured the Count of Flanders — the countess, like a prudent matron, is thinking of marriages for her children — and has sent him three hundred ells of linen to make shirts. The Archbishop of Rheims is the count's dear friend. . . . . I advise you, therefore, to trust in God and give yourself to prayer. Put away thoughts of this world; pray

---

[1] "Sed et citius poterit apostolica circumveniri religio ex varietate verborum regis . . . . et si rex infirmiora domini papæ prænoverit exitus viarum suarum obstruet offendiculis." — *Materials,* vol. ii. p. 346.

and meditate. The Psalms will be better reading for you than philosophy; and to confer with spiritual men, whose example may influence your devotion, will profit you more than indulging in litigious speculations. I say this from my heart: take it as you please.

These words show Becket to us as through an inverted telescope, the magnifying mist blown away, in his true outlines and true proportions. The true Becket, as the pope knew him, was not the person peculiarly fitted to be the Church's champion in a cause which was really sacred. John of Salisbury thought evidently at this time that there was no longer any hope that the archbishop would really succeed. He wished, he said in a letter to the Bishop of Exeter, to make his peace with the king. He could not desert the archbishop, but he was loyal to his sovereign. He called God to witness how often he had rebuked the . archbishop for his foolish violence.[1] He could not promise that he would quit his old master's service, but in all else he would be guided by the Bishop of Exeter's advice.

---

1 " Novit enim cordium inspector quod sæpius et asperius quam aliquis mortalium corripuerim dominum archiepiscopum de his in quibus ab initio dominum regem et suos zelo quodam inconsultius visus est ad amaritudinem provocàsse," etc. — Letters, vol. i. p. 203, ed. Giles.

CHAPTER VI.

MEANWHILE the quarrel between Becket and the King of England became the topic of the hour throughout Europe. Which was right and which was wrong, what the pope would do or ought to do, and whether England would join Germany in the schism — these questions were the theme of perpetual discussions in council and conclave, were debated in universities, and were fought over at convent and castle dinner-tables. Opinions were so divided that, in a cause which concerned Heaven so nearly, people were looking for Heaven to give some sign. As facts were wanting, legend took the place of them, and stories began to spread, either at the time or immediately after, of direct and picturesque manifestations of grace which had been vouchsafed in Becket's favor. It was said that when dining with Pope Aléxander he had twice unconsciously turned water into wine. At Pontigny he had been graciously visited by our Lady herself. He had left England ill provided with clothes. His wardrobe was in disorder; his drawers especially, besides being dirty, were in holes. He was specially delicate in such matters, and was too modest to confess his difficulties. He stayed at home one day alone to do the repairs himself. He was pricking his fingers and succeeding indifferently, when our Lady — who, as the biographers tell us, had been taught to sew when she was at Nazareth — came in, sat down, took the drawers out of the archbishop's hand, mended them excellently, and went as she had come. The archbishop had not recognized his visitor. Soon after a singular case of church discipline was referred to his decision. A young Frenchman, specially devoted to the Virgin Mary, had built a chapel in her honor not far from Pontigny, had placed her image over the altar, and had obtained ordination himself that he might make his daily offerings there. But he neither would nor could repeat any mass but the mass of the Virgin. The authorities reprimanded him but to no purpose. Our Lady filled his soul, and left no room for any other object. The irregularity was flagrant — the devotion was commendable. Becket was consulted as to what should be done, and Becket sent for the offender and gently put before him that he was making a scandal which must positively cease. The youth rushed away in despair, and flung himself before our Lady's image, declaring that his love was for her and for her alone. She must save him from interference, or he would pull the chapel down and do other wild and desperate things. The eyes of the image began to smile, the neck bent, the lips opened. "Have no fear, *carissime*," it said : " go to the archbishop. Entreat again to be allowed to continue your devotions to me. If he refuses, ask him if he remembers who mended his drawers." We may guess how the story ended.

With tales of this kind floating in the air, the first year of Becket's exile wore out, the pope giving uncertain answers to the passionate appeals which continued to be made to him, according to the fortune of the Emperor Frederick in Italy. Frederick being at last driven out of Lombardy, the pope recovered heart, and held out brighter prospects. He sent Becket permission to excommunicate the persons in occupation of his estates and benefices, and he promised to ratify his sentence if opportunely issued. He did not permit, but also did not specially forbid, him to excommunicate the king, while Lewis, with Becket's knowledge, and in the opinion of the cardinals who came afterwards to inquire into his conduct, at Becket's direct instigation, prepared to invade Normandy. Henry, well informed of what was coming, began now to turn to Germany in earnest. By the advice of his barons, as he said, he wrote to Reginald, Frederick's archbishop chancellor, to tell him that he was about to send an embassy to the pope to demand that he should be relieved of Becket, and that the Constitutions should be ratified. If justice was refused him, he and his people were prepared to renounce their allegiance to Alexander and to unite with Germany.[1] The chancellor was himself invited to England to arrange a marriage between the Princess Matilda and the Duke of Saxony. A decided step of this kind it was thought might bring the pope to his senses.

Separation from Rome, indeed, was the true alternative: and had the country been prepared to follow Henry, and had Henry himself been prepared at the bottom of his mind to defy the pope and the worst that he could do, the great schism between the Teutonic and Latin races might have been antedated, and the course of history been changed. But Henry was threatening with but half a heart, and the country was less prepared than he. In Germany itself, the pope in the end proved too strong for the emperor. In England, even Wickliffe was premature. With all its enormous faults, the Roman Catholic organization in both countries was producing better fruits on the whole than any other which could have been substituted for it; and almost three centuries had yet to pass, bringing with them accumulating masses of insincerities and injustices, before Europe could become ripe for a change. A succession of Beckets would have precipitated a rupture, whatever might be the cost or consequences; but the succeeding prelates were men of the world as well as statesmen, and were too wise to press theories to their logical consequences.

The Archbishop of Cologne came to London with the taint of his schism upon him. The court entertained him. The German marriage was arranged. But Henry received a startling intimation that he must not try the barons too

1 Giles, vol. i. p. 316.

far. They had supported him in what they held to be reasonable demands to which the pope might be expected to consent. They were not ready to support him in a revolt from Rome, even though disguised behind the name of an antipope. The hunchbacked Earl of Leicester refused Barbarossa's chancellor the kiss of peace in open court at Westminster, and on his departure the altars at which the schismatic prelate had said mass were destroyed.[1]

Alexander meanwhile had written to Foliot, directing him and the Bishop of Hereford to remonstrate with the king, to entreat him to act in conformity with his past reputation and to put an end to the scandal which he had caused, hinting that if Henry persisted in refusing he might be unable to restrain the archbishop from excommunicating him. The two bishops discharged their commission. "The king," Foliot replied to the pope, "took what we said in excellent part. He assured us that his affection towards your holiness remained as it had been, but he said that he had stood by you in your misfortunes, and that he had met with a bad return. He had hindered no one from going to you on your invitation, and he meant to hinder no one. As to appeals, he merely claimed that each case should be first thoroughly heard in his own courts. If justice could not be had there, appeals to Rome might remain without objection from himself. If the emperor was excommunicated, he promised to break off correspondence with him. As to the Archbishop of Canterbury, he had not been expelled from England; he had left it of his own accord, and might return when he pleased. To the Church, now as always, he wished to submit his differences with the archbishop."

If this was not all which the pope might expect, Foliot advised him to be contented with it. "The king," he continued, "having consented to defer to the Church, considers that right is on his side. Let your holiness therefore beware of measures which may drive him and his subjects into

[1] Matthew Paris, *Chronica Majora*, 1165.

revolt. A wounded limb may be healed ; a limb cut off is lost forever. Some of us may bear persecution on your account, but there will not be wanting those who will bow their knee to Baal. Men can be found to fill the English sees who will obey the antipope. Many, indeed, already wish for the change." [1]

The pope, who did not understand the English character, was as much disturbed as Henry could have desired to see him. He found that he had encouraged Becket too far. He wrote to press upon him that the days were evil ; that he must endeavor to conciliate the king; that he must on no account excommunicate him, or lay England under interdict, or venture any violent courses, at any rate before the ensuing Easter. [2] He wrote affectionately to Henry himself. He thanked the two bishops with the utmost warmth, and expressed himself delighted with the accounts which he received of the king's frame of mind. [3] The Archbishop of Rouen and the Empress Matilda had written to him to the same purpose, and had given him equal pleasure. If Foliot could bring about a reconciliation, he would love him forever. Meanwhile he would follow Foliot's advice and keep Becket quiet.

A very slight concession from Becket would now have made an arrangement possible, for Henry was tired of the quarrel. He invited the Norman prelates to meet him at a conference at Chinon. The archbishop was expected to attend, and peace was then to have been arranged. In this spirit the Bishop of Hereford addressed the archbishop himself, entreating him to agree to moderate conditions. Far away was Becket from concessions. He knew better than the pope the state of English feeling. He was in correspondence (it is likely enough) with the Earl of Leicester. At all events he must have heard of Leicester's treatment

---

[1] Foliot to the Pope, 1165. Hoveden (ed. Giles), vol. i. p. 231.
[2] Giles, vol. i. p. 324.
[3] " Gaudemus et exultamus super eâ devotione ejusdem regis."

of Reginald of Cologne. He knew that in fearing that England would go into schism the pope was frightened by a shadow. He had not defied king, peers, and bishops at Northampton that the fight should end in a miserable compromise. Sharply he rebuked the Bishop of Hereford for his timid counsels. " For you," he said, " I am made anathema, and when you should stand by me you advise me to yield. You should rather have bidden me draw the sword of Peter and avenge the blood of the saints. I mourn over you as over my firstborn. Up, my son. Cry aloud and cease not. Lift up your voice, lest God's anger fall on you and all the nation perish. I grieve for the king. Tribulation impends over him. They have devoured Jacob and laid waste his dwelling-place." [1]

To John of Salisbury Becket announced that his patience was exhausted, that when Easter was passed he would be free, and that in his own opinion he ought to forbear no longer. He desired to know how far his friend agreed with him. John of Salisbury was more prudent than his master. " Precipitate action," he said, " may expose you to ridicule and ruin. You ask my advice. I recommend you not to rely on the Holy See. Write to the empress mother, write to the Archbishop of Rouen and the other prelates. Tell them you are ready to obey the law and go back if you are treated with justice. The adversary will not agree to conditions really fair, but you will have set yourself right with the world. Should the king be more moderate than I think he will be, do not stand upon securities. Content yourself with a promise under the king's hand and the assurance of the empress mother. Do not try the censures. You know my opinion about this, and you once agreed with me. The king is not afraid of excommunication. The bishops and most of the clergy have stood by him; some may be with us in heart, but they are not to be depended on." [2]

---

[1] Becket to the Bishop of Hereford, Hoveden. I am obliged greatly to compress the diffuse rhetoric of the archbishop.

[2] John of Salisbury to Becket, April, 1166 (abridged).

Becket, like most persons of his temperament, asked advice without meaning to follow it. He addressed the king in a letter which Herbert describes as being of extreme sweetness. It was to entreat him to let loose the bride of Christ whom he held in captivity, and to warn him that if he persevered in his wicked ways, "Christ would gird his sword upon his thigh," and would descend from heaven to punish him. Inflated language of this kind was not general at that time. It was peculiar to Becket, and we need not be surprised that it produced no effect on Henry. He went to Normandy to the Chinon conference immediately after Easter, 1166, hoping there to meet Becket and speak with him and with the other prelates as with reasonable men. He did not find Becket there, but he found a second letter from him, which from a saint would have tried the temper of a more patient sovereign than Henry, and from a man whom he had known so lately as a defaulting chancellor and unscrupulous politician was insolent and absurd. After reproaching the king for allowing him to live on the charity of Lewis of France, the archbishop proceeded : —

You are my king, my lord, and my spiritual son. As you are my king, I owe you reverence and admonition; as you are my lord, I owe you such obedience as consists with the honor of God; as you are my son, I owe you the chastisement which is due from the father to the child. You hold your authority from the Church, which consists of clergy and laymen. The clergy have sole charge of things spiritual : kings, earls, and counts have powers delegated to them from the Church, to preserve peace and the Church's unity. Delegated from the Church, I say. Therefore it rests not with you to tell bishops whom they may excommunicate, or to force clergy to their answers in secular courts, or to interfere with tithes, or do any of those things to which you pretend in the name of custom. Remember your coronation oath. Restore my property. Allow me to return to Canterbury, and I will obey you as far as the honor of God and the Holy See and our sacred order permits me. Refuse, and be assured you will not fail to experience the severe displeasure of Almighty God.[1]

This letter appears to have been placed in Henry's hands immediately before he met the Norman bishops. On entering the conference he was ill with agitation. Persons present said that he was in tears. He told the bishops that Becket was aiming at his destruction, soul and body. He said they were no better than traitors for not protecting him more effectually from the violence of a single man.[2] The Archbishop of Rouen protested against the word "traitors." But it was no time for niceties of expression. War with France was on the point of breaking out, and Becket, it was now plain, meant to give it the character of a sacred war by excommunicating Henry. Easter was past: he was free to act, and clearly enough he meant to act. The Bishop of Lisieux advised an instant appeal to the pope, which would keep Becket's hands tied for the moment. He and another bishop rushed off to Pontigny to serve the notice on him. They arrived too late. Before launching his thunderbolts Becket had gone to Soissons, there to prepare for the operation.

At Soissons were to be found in special presence the Blessed Virgin and St. Gregory, whose assistance the archbishop considered would be peculiarly valuable to him ; and not they only, but another saint, Beatus Drausius, the patron of pugilists and duellists, who promised victory to intending combatants on their passing a night at his shrine.[3]

[1] Becket to the King, May, 1166 (abridged).

[2] "Tandem dixit quod omnes proditores erant, qui eum adhibitâ operâ et diligentiâ ab unius hominis infestatione nolebant impedire."

[3] "Archiepiscopus noster in procinctu ferendæ sententiæ constitutus iter arripuerat ad urbem Suessionum orationis causâ, ut Beatæ Virgini, cujus ibi memoria celebris est, et Beato Drausio, ad quem confugiunt pugnaturi, et Beato Gregorio Anglicanæ Ecclesiæ fundatori, qui in eâdem urbe requiescit, agonem suum precibus commendaret. Est autem Beatus Drausius gloriosissimus confessor qui, sicut Franci et Lotharingi credunt, pugiles qui ad memoriam ejus pernoctant reddit invictos." — John of Salisbury to the Bishop of Exeter. Letters, vol. i. p. 227, ed. Giles.

Becket gave St. Drausius three nights — or perhaps one
to each saint — and thus fortified he betook himself to
Vezelay, where at Whitsuntide vast numbers of people
assembled from all parts of France.   There from the pulpit
after sermon on Whitsuntide, with the appropriate ceremonies of bells and lighted candles quenched, he took vengeance at last upon his enemies.   He suspended the Bishop
of Salisbury.   He cursed John of Oxford and the Archdeacon of Ilchester, two leading churchmen of the king's
party.   He cursed Chief Justice de Luci, who had directed
the sequestration of his see.   He cursed Ranulf de Broc
and every person employed in administering his estates.
Finally he cursed every one who maintained the Constitutions of Clarendon, and he released the bishops from their
promise to observe them.   A remnant of prudence or a report of the king's illness led him partially to withhold his
hand.   He did not actually curse Henry, but he threatened
that he shortly would curse him unless he repented,

In high delight with himself the archbishop issued a
pastoral to the bishops of England telling them what he
had done, talking in his usual high style of the rights of
priests over kings and princes, and ordering them at their
souls' peril to see that the sentence was obeyed.   He wrote
at the same time to the pope inclosing the terms of the
excommunication, his condemnation of the Constitutions,
and the threats which he had addressed to the king.   These
threats he declared his intention of carrying into effect unless the king showed speedy signs of submission, and he
required Alexander in a tone of imperious consequence to
confirm what he had done.

On the arrival of the censures in England the bishops
met in London and determined on a further appeal to the
pope.   They addressed a unanimous and remarkable re-
monstrance to him, going into the origin of the quarrel, insisting on the abominable conduct of many of the clergy,
the necessity of reform, and the moderation which the king

had shown.[1] The Constitutions which he had adopted they declared to have been taken from the established customs of the realm. If they appeared objectionable, his holiness need but point to the articles of which he disapproved, and they should be immediately altered. The archbishop's uncalled-for violence had been the sole obstacle to an arrangement.

With this letter and others from the king an embassy was dispatched to Rome, John of Oxford, whom Becket had personally excommunicated, being significantly one of its members.

Pending the result of the appeal, the English bishops in a body remonstrated with Becket himself. They reminded him of his personal obligations to the king, and of the dangers which he was provoking. The king, they said, had listened coldly hitherto to the advances of Germany. But these good dispositions might not last forever. For the archbishop to scatter curses without allowing the persons denounced an opportunity of answering for themselves, was against reason and precedent; and they had placed themselves under the protection of his holiness.

Becket was not to be frightened by threats of German alliance. He knew better. He lectured the bishops for their want of understanding. He rebuked them for their cowardice and want of faith. The Bishop of London had recalled to him unpleasant passages in his own past history. The tone of Foliot as well as his person drove Becket wild. He spoke of the Bishop of London as an Ahitophel and a Doeg.

Your letter (he replied to him) is like a scorpion with a sting in its tail. You profess obedience to me, and to avoid obedience you appeal to the pope. Little will you gain by it. You have no feeling for me, or for the Church, or for the king, whose

---

1 " Qui cum pacem regni sui enormi insolentium quorundam clericorum excessu non mediocriter turbari cognosceret, clero debitam exhibens reverentiam eorundem excessus ad ecclesiæ judices retulit episcopos, ut gladius gladio subveniat." — *Ad Alexandrum Pontificem.* Hoveden, vol. i. p. 266.

soul is perishing. You blame me for threatening him. What father will see his son go astray and hesitate to restrain that son? Who will not use the rod that he may spare the sword? The ship is in the storm : I am at the helm, and you bid me sleep. To him who speaks thus to me I reply, " Get thee behind me, Satan!" The king, you say, desires to do what is right. My clergy are banished, my possessions are taken from me, the sword hangs over my neck. Do you call this right? Tell the king that the Lord of men and angels has established two powers, princes and priests — the first earthly, the second spiritual; the first to obey, the second to command. He who breaks this order breaks the ordinance of God. Tell him it is no dishonor to him to submit to those to whom God himself defers, calling them gods in the sacred writings. For thus he speaks: " I have said ye are gods; " and again, " I will make thee a God unto Pharaoh;" " Thou shalt take nothing from the gods " (*i. e.* the priests).[1] . . . . The king may not judge his judges; the lips of the priest shall keep wisdom. It is written, " Thou shalt require the law at his mouth, for he is the angel of God."

The Catholic Church would have had but a brief career in this world if the rulers of it had been so wild of mind as this astonishing martyr of Canterbury. The air-bubble, when blown the fullest and shining the brightest, is nearest to collapsing into a drop of dirty water. John of Salisbury, sympathizing with him and admiring him as he generally did, saw clearly that the pope could never sanction so preposterous an attitude. " I have little trust in the Church of Rome," he said. " I know the ways of it and the needs of it too well. So greedy, so dishonest are the Romans, that they use too often the license of power, and take dispensations to grant what they say is useful to the commonwealth, however fatal it may be to religion." [2]

[1] "Non indignetur itaque dominus noster deferre illis quibus omnium Summus deferre non dedignatur, deos appellans eos sæpius in sacris literis. Sic enim dicit, 'Ego dixi, Dii estis,' etc.; et iterum, 'Constitui te deum Pharaonis,' 'Et diis non detrahes,' *i. e.* sacerdotibus," etc. — Becket to Foliot. Hoveden, vol. i. p. 261.

[2] "Nec de ecclesiâ Romanâ, cujus mores et necessitates nobis innotu-

The first practical effect of the excommunication was the recoil of the blow upon the archbishop's entertainers. In the shelter of a Cistercian abbey in France, an English subject was committing treason and levying war against his sovereign and his country. A chapter of the Cistercian Order was held in September. King Henry sent a message to the general, that, if his abbot continued to protect Becket, the Cistercians in England would be suppressed, and their property confiscated. The startled general did not dare to resist; a message was sent to Pontigny; in the fluttered dovecote it was resolved that Becket must go, and it was a cruel moment to him. A fresh asylum was provided for him at Sens. But he had grown accustomed to Pontigny, and had led a pleasant life there. On his first arrival he had attempted asceticisms, but his health had suffered, and his severities had been relaxed. He was out of spirits at his departure. His tears were flowing. The abbot cheered him up, laughed at his dejection, and told him there was nothing in his fate so particularly terrible. Becket said that he had dreamt the night before that he was to be martyred. "Martyrdom!" laughed the abbot; "what has a man who eats and drinks like you to do with martyrdom? The cup of wine which you drink has small affinity with the cup of martyrdom." "I confess," said Becket, "that I indulge in pleasures of the flesh. Yet the good God has deigned to reveal my fate to me." [1]

Sad at heart, the archbishop removed to Sens; yet if the pope stood firm, all might yet be well.

erunt, multum confido. Tot et tantæ sunt necessitates, tanta aviditas et improbitas Romanorum, ut interdum utatur licentiâ potestatis, procuretque ex dispensatione quod reipublicæ dicitur expedire, etsi non expediat religioni." — To Becket. Letters, 1166.

[1] "'Ergo martyrio interibis? Quid esculento et temulento et martyri? Non bene conveniunt, nec in unâ sede morantur, calix vini quod potas et calix martyrii.' 'Fateor,' inquit, 'corporeis voluptatibus indulgeo. Bonus tamen Dominus, qui justificat impium, indigno dignatus est revelare mysterium.'" — *Materials*, vol. i. p. 51.

CHAPTER VII.

THE archbishop's letters show conclusively that the Constitutions were not the real causes of the dispute with the king. The king was willing to leave the Constitutions to be modified by the pope. The archbishop's contest, lying concealed in his favorite phrases, "saving my order," "saving the honor of God," was for the supremacy of the Church over the Crown; for the degradation of the civil power into the position of delegate of the pope and bishops. All authority was derived from God. The clergy were the direct ministers of God. Therefore all authority was derived from God through them. However well the assumption might appear in theory, it would not work in practice, and John of Salisbury was right iu concluding that the pope would never sanction an assumption which, broadly stated and really acted on, would shake the fabric of the Church throughout Europe. Alexander was dreaming of peace when the news reached him of the excommunications at Vezelay. The news that Chief Justice de Luci had hanged 500 felonious clerks in England would have caused him less annoyance. Henry's envoys brought with them the bishops' appeal, and renewed the demand for cardinal legates to be sent to end the quarrel. This time the pope decided that the legates should go, carrying with them powers to take off Becket's censures. He prohibited Becket himself from pursuing his threats further till the cardinals' arrival. To Henry he sent a private letter — which, however, he permitted him to show if circumstances made it necessary — declaring beforehand that any sentences which the archbishop might issue against himself or his subjects should be void.[1]

The humiliation was terrible ; Becket's victims were free, and even rewarded. John of Oxford came back from Rome with the Deanery of Salisbury. Worst of all, the cardinals were coming, and those the most dreaded of the whole body, Cardinal Otho and Cardinal William of Pavia. One of them, said John of Salisbury, was light and uncertain, the other crafty and false, and both made up of avarice. These were the ministers of the Holy See, for whose pretensions Becket was fighting. This was his estimate of them when they were to try his own cause. His letters at this moment were filled with despair. " Ridicule has fallen on me," he said, " and shame on the pope. I am to be obeyed no longer. I am betrayed and given to destruction. My deposition is a settled thing. Of this, at least, let the pope assure himself: never will I accept the Cardinal of Pavia for my judge. When they are rid of me, I hear he is to be my successor at Canterbury."[2]

Becket, however, was not the man to leave the field while life was in him. There was still hope, for war had broken out at last, and Henry and Lewis were killing and burning in each other's territories. If not the instigator, Becket was the occasion, and Lewis, for his own interests, would still be forced to stand by him. He was intensely superstitious. His cause, he was convinced, was God's cause. Hitherto God had allowed him to fail on account of his own deficiencies, and the deficiencies required to be amended. Like certain persons who cut themselves with knives and lancets, he determined now to mortify his flesh in earnest. When settled in his new life at Sens, he rose at daybreak, prayed in his oratory, said mass, and prayed and wept again. Five times each day and night his chaplain flogged him. His food was bread and water, his bed the floor. A hair shirt

---

[1] The Pope to Henry, December 20, 1166.
[2] Becket's Letters, Giles, vol. ii. p. 60.

was not enough without hair drawers which reached his knees, and both were worn till they swarmed with vermin.[1] The cardinals approached, and the prospect grew hourly blacker. The pope rebuked Lewis for the war. The opportunity of the cardinals' presence was to be used for restoration of peace. Poor as Becket was, he could not approach these holy beings on their accessible side. "The Cardinal of Pavia," said John of Salisbury, "thinks only of the king's money, and has no fear of God in him. Cardinal Otho is better: *Romanus tamen et cardinalis* (but he is a Roman and a cardinal). If we submit our cause to them, we lose it to a certainty. If we refuse we offend the King of France." The Cardinal of Pavia wrote to announce to Becket his arrival in France and the purpose of his mission. Becket replied with a violent letter, of which he sent a copy to John of Salisbury, but dispatched it before his friend could stop him. John of Salisbury thought that the archbishop had lost his senses. "Compare the cardinal's letter and your answer to it," he said. "What had the cardinal done that you should tell him he was giving you poison? You have no right to insult a cardinal and the pope's legate on his first communication with you. Were he to send your letter to Rome, you might be charged with contumacy. He tells you he is come to close the dispute to the honor of God and the Church. What poison is there in this? He is not to blame because he cautions you not to provoke the king further. Your best friends have often given you the same advice."

With great difficulty Becket was brought to consent to

---

[1] Myths gathered about the state of these garments. One day, we are told, he was dining with the Queen of France. She observed that his sleeves were fastened unusually tightly at the wrist, and that something moved inside them. He tried to evade her curiosity, for the moving things were maggots. But she pressed her questions till he was obliged to loosen the strings. Pearls of choicest size and color rolled upon the table. The queen wished to keep one, but it could not be. The pearls were restored to the sleeve, and became maggots as before. — *Materials*, vol. ii. p. 296.

see the cardinals. They came to him at Sens, but stayed for a short time only, and went on to the king in Normandy. The archbishop gathered no comfort from his speech with them. He took to his bell and candles again, and cursed the Bishop of London. He still intended to curse the king and declare an interdict. He wrote to a friend, Cardinal Hyacinth, at Rome, to say that he would never submit to the arbitration of the cardinal legates, and bidding him urge the pope to confirm the sentences which he was about to pronounce.[1] He implored the pope himself to recall the cardinals and unsheath the sword of Peter. To his entire confusion, he learned that the king held a letter from the pope declaring that his curses would be so much wasted breath.

The pope tried to soothe him. Soft words cost Alexander nothing ; and, while protecting Henry from spiritual thunders, he assured the archbishop himself that his power should not be taken from him. Nor, indeed, had the violence of Becket's agitation any real occasion. Alexander wished to frighten him into submission, but had no intention of compromising himself by an authoritative decision. Many months passed away, and Becket still refused to plead before the cardinals. At length they let out that their powers extended no further than advice, and Becket, thus satisfied, consented to an official conference. The meeting was held near Gisors, on the frontiers of France and Normandy, on the 18th of November, 1167. The archbishop came attended by his exiled English friends. With the cardinals were a large body of Norman bishops and abbots. The cardinals, earnest for peace if they could bring their refractory patient to consent to it, laid before him the general unfitness of the quarrel. They accused him of ingratitude, of want of loyalty to his sovereign, and, among other things, of having instigated the war.[2]

[1] Giles, vol. ii. p. 86.

[2] "Imponens ei inter cætera quod excitaverat guerram regis Franco-
rum." — *Materials*, vol. i. p. 66.

The last charge the archbishop sharply denied, and Lewis afterwards acquitted him also. For the rest he said that the king had begun by attacking the Church. He was willing to consent to any reasonable terms of arrangement, with security for God's honor, proper respect for himself, and the restoration of his estates. They asked if he would recognize the Constitutions; he said that no such engagement had been required of his predecessors, and ought not to be required of him. "The book of abominations," as he called the Constitutions, was produced and read, and he challenged the cardinals to affirm that Christian men should obey such laws.

Henry was prepared to accept the smallest concession; nothing need be said about the Constitutions if Becket would go back to Canterbury, resume his duties, and give a general promise to be quiet. The archbishop answered that there was a proverb in England that silence gave consent. The question had been raised, and could not now be passed over. The cardinals asked if he would accept their judgment on the whole cause. He said that he would go into court before them or any one whom the pope might appoint, as soon as his property was restored to him. In his present poverty he could not encounter the expense of a lawsuit.

Curious satire on Becket's whole contention, none the less so that he was himself unconscious of the absurdity! He withdrew from the conference, believing that he had gained a victory, and he again began to meditate drawing his spiritual sword. Messengers on all sides again flew off to Rome, from the king and English bishops, from the cardinals, from Becket himself. The king and bishops placed themselves under the pope's protection should the archbishop begin his curses. The Constitutions were once more placed at the pope's discretion to modify at his pleasure. The cardinals wrote charging Becket with being the sole cause of the continuance of the quarrel, and, in spite of his denials, persisting in accusing him of having caused the war. Becket prayed again for the cardinals' recall, and for the pope's sanction of more vigorous action.

He had not yet done with the cardinals ; they knew him, and they knew his restless humor. Pending fresh resolutions from Rome, they suspended him, and left him incapable either of excommunicating or exercising any other function of spiritual authority whatsoever. Once more he was plunged into despair.

Through those legates, he cried in his anguish to the pope, "We are made a derision to those about us. My lord, have pity on me. You are my refuge. I can scarcely breathe for anguish. My harp is turned to mourning, and my joy to sadness. The last error is worse than the first."

The pope seemed deaf to his lamentations. The suspension was not removed. Plans were formed for his translation from Canterbury to some other preferment. He said he would rather be killed. The pope wrote so graciously to Henry that the king said he for the first time felt that he was sovereign in his own realm. John of Salisbury's mournful conviction was that the game was at last played out. "We know those Romans," he sighed : "*qui munere potentior est, potentior est jure.* The antipope could not have done more for the king than they have done. It will be written in the annals of the Holy See that the herald of truth, the champion of liberty, the preacher of the law of the Lord, has been deprived and treated as a criminal at the threats of an English prince."

It is hard to say what influence again turned the scale. Perhaps Alexander was encouraged by the failures of Barbarossa in Italy. Perhaps Henry had been too triumphant, and had irritated the pope and cardinals by producing their letters, and speaking too frankly of the influences by which the holy men had been bound to his side.[1] In accepting Henry's money they had not bargained for exposure. They

[1] John of Salisbury, Letters, vol. ii. p. 144, ed. Giles

were ashamed and sore, and Becket grew again into favor. The pope at the end of 1168 gave him back his powers, permitting him to excommunicate even Henry himself unless he repented before the ensuing Easter. The legates were recalled as Becket desired. Cardinal Otho recommended the king to make his peace on the best terms which he could get. John of Salisbury, less confident, but with amused contempt of the chameleonlike Alexander, advised Henry, through the Bishop of Poitiers, to treat with the archbishop immediately, *nec mediante Romano episcopo, nec rege Franciæ nec operâ cardinalium*, without help either of pope, of French king or cardinals. Since Becket could not be frightened, Alexander was perhaps trying what could be done with Henry; but he was as eager as any one for an end of some kind to a business which was now adding disgrace and scandal to its other mischiefs. Peace was arranged at last between Lewis and Henry. The English king gave up a point for which he had long contended, and consented to do homage for Normandy and Anjou. The day after Epiphany, January 7, 1169, the two princes met at Montmirail, between Chartres and Le Mans, attended by their peers and prelates.

In the general pacification the central disturber was, if possible, to be included. The pope had sent commissioners, as we should call them — Simon, prior of Montdieu, Engelbert, prior of Val St. Pierre, and Bernard de Corilo — to advise and, if possible, guide Becket into wiser courses. The political ceremonies were accomplished, Lewis and Henry were reconciled amidst general satisfaction and enthusiasm. Becket was then introduced, led in by the Archbishop of Sens, the son of the aged Theobald, Count of Blois. Henry and he had not met since the Northampton council. He threw himself in apparent humility at the king's feet. " My lord," he said, " I ask you to forgive me. I place myself in God's hands and in yours." [1] At a pre-

---

[1] " Miserere mei, domine, quia pono me in Deo et vobis ad honorem Dei et vestrûm."

liminary meeting the pope's envoys and the French clergy
had urged him to submit without conditions. He had insisted on his usual reservation, but they had objected to
saving clauses. He seemed now inclined really to yield, so
Herbert de Bosham says, and Herbert whispered to him to
stand firm.

"My lord king," said Henry, after Becket had made his
general submission, "and you my lords and prelates, what I
require of the archbishop is no more than that he will observe the laws which have been observed by his predecessors. I ask him now to give me that promise." Becket no
longer answered with the reservation of his order: he
changed the phrase. He promised obedience, saving the
honor of God.

"You wish," replied Henry, powerfully disappointed and
displeased, "to be king in my place. This man," he continued, turning to Lewis, "deserted his Church of his own
will, and he tells you and all men that his cause is the cause
of the Church. He has governed his Church with as much
freedom as those who have gone before him, but now he
stands on God's honor to oppose me wherever he pleases,
as if I cared for God's honor less than he. I make this
proposal. Many kings have ruled in England before me,
some less, some greater than I am; many holy men have
been Archbishops of Canterbury before him. Let him be-
have to me as the most sainted of his predecessors behaved
to the least worthy of mine, and I am content."

The king's demand seemed just and moderate to all present.[1] The archbishop hesitated. Lewis asked him if he
aspired to be greater than acknowledged saints. His predecessors, he said, had extirpated some abuses but not all.
There was work which remained to be done. He was
stopped by a general outcry that the king had yielded
enough; the saving clause must be dropped. At once, at
the tone of command, Becket's spirit rose. Priests and

1 " Rem justam et modestam visus est omnibus postulare."

bishops, he answered defiantly, were not to submit to men of this world save with reservations; he for one would not do it.

The meeting broke up in confusion. A French noble said that the archbishop was abusing their hospitality, and did not deserve any longer protection. Henry mounted his horse and rode sadly away. The pope's agents followed him, wringing their hands and begging for some slight additional concession. The king told them that they must address themselves to the archbishop, Let the archbishop bind himself to obey the laws. If the laws were amiss, they should be modified by the pope's wishes. In no country in the world, he said, had the clergy so much liberty as in England, and in no country were there greater villains among them. For the sake of peace he did not insist on terms precisely defined. The archbishop was required to do nothing beyond what had been done by Anselm.

Becket, however, was again immovable as stone. Lewis, after a brief coldness, took him back into favor. His power of cursing had been restored to him. The doubt was only whether the pope had recalled the safeguards which he had given to the king. The pope's agents, on the failure of the conference, gave Henry a second letter, in which Alexander told him that, unless peace was made, he could not restrain the archbishop longer. Again representatives of the various parties hurried off to Rome, Becket insisting that if the pope would only be firm the king would yield, Henry embarrassing the pope more completely than threats of schism could have done by placing the Constitutions unreservedly in his hands, and binding himself to adopt any change which the pope might suggest. Becket, feverish and impatient, would not wait for the pope's decision, and preferred to force his hand by action. He summoned the Bishops of London and Salisbury to appear before him. They appealed to Rome, but their appeal was disregarded. Appeals, as Becket characteristically said, were not allowed in order

to shield the guilty, but to protect the innocent. On Palm
Sunday, at Clairvaux, he took once more to his bell and
candles. He excommunicated the two bishops and every
one who had been concerned with his property — the Earl
of Norfolk, Sir Ranulf de Broc, whom he peculiarly hated,
Robert de Broc, and various other persons. The chief
justice he threatened. The king he still left unmentioned,
for fear of provoking the pope too far.

Harassed on both sides, knowing perfectly well on which
side good sense and justice lay, yet not daring to declare
Becket wrong, and accept what, after all that had passed,
would be construed into a defeat of the Church, the unfortunate Alexander drifted on as he best could, writing letters
in one sense one day and contradicting them the next. On
the surface he seemed hopelessly false. The falsehood was
no more than weakness, a specious anxiety to please the
king without offending the archbishop, and trusting to time
and weariness to bring about an end. There is no occasion
to follow the details of his duplicities. Two legates were
again sent — not cardinals this time, but ecclesiastical law-
yers, Gratian and Vivian — bound by oath this time to
cause no scandal by accepting bribes. As usual, the choice
was impartial ; Gratian for Becket, Vivian for the king.
So long as his excommunications were allowed to stand,
Becket cared little who might come. He added the chief
justice to the list of the accursed, as he had threatened to do.
He wrote to the Bishop of Ostia that the king's disposition
could only be amended by punishment. The serpent head
of the iniquity must now be bruised, and he bade the bishop
impress the necessity of it upon the pope. Gratian was
taken into Becket's confidence. Vivian he treated coldly
and contemptuously. According to Herbert and Becket's
friends, Gratian reported that the king was shifty and false,
and that his object was to betray the Church and the archbishop. Henry himself declared that he assented to all that
they proposed to him, and Diceto says that the legates were

on the point of giving judgment in Henry's favor when the
Archbishop of Sens interposed and forbade them.   In thé
confusion of statement the actions of either party alone can
be usefully attended to, and behind the acts of all, or at
least of the pope, there was the usual ambiguity.   Alexander
threatened the king.   He again empowered Becket to use
whatever power he possessed to bring him to submission,
and he promised to confirm his sentences.[1]   As certainly he
had secret conferences at Rome with Henry's envoys, and
promised, on the other hand, that the archbishop should not
be allowed to hurt him.   Becket, furious and uncontrollable,
called the Bishop of London a parricide, an infidel, a Go-
liath, a son of Belial ; he charged the Bishop of Hereford
to see that the sentence against Foliot and his brother of
Salisbury should be observed in England.   Henry, on the
other hand, assured Foliot of protection, and sent him to
Rome with letters from himself to pursue his appeal and
receive absolution from the pope himself.   The Count of
Flanders interposed, the Count of Mayence interposed, but
without effect.   At length on the 18th of November, the
anniversary of the conference with the cardinals at Gisors,
Henry and Lewis met again at Montmartre outside Paris,
Becket and his friends being in attendance in an adjoining
chapel.   Gratian had returned to Rome.   Vivian was present, and pressed Lewis to bring the archbishop to reason.
Lewis really exerted himself, and not entirely unsuccess-
fully.   Henry was even more moderate than before.   The
Constitutions, by the confession of Becket's biographer,
Herbert, who was with him on the spot, were practically
abandoned. Henry's only condition was that the archbishop
should not usurp the functions of the civil power ; he, on
his part, undertaking not to strain the prerogative.   Becket
dropped his saving clause, and consented to make the promise required of him, if the king would restore his estates,
and give him compensation for the arrear rents, which he

[1] " Quod ea quæ statuerit non mutabuntur.''

estimated at 20,000*l.* Lewis said that money ought not to
be an obstacle to peace. It was unworthy of the archbishop
to raise so poor a difficulty. But here, too, Henry gave
way. An impartial estimate should be made, and Becket
was to be repaid.

But now, no more than before, had the archbishop any
real intention of submitting. His only fear was of offending Lewis. The Archbishop of Sens had gone to Rome to
persuade the pope to give him legatine powers over Henry's French dominions. The censures of the Church might
be resisted in England. If Normandy, Anjou, and Aquitaine were laid under interdict, these two spiritual conspir-
ators had concluded that the king would be forced to surrender. Becket was daily expecting a favorable answer,
and meanwhile was protracting the time. He demanded
guarantees. He did not suspect the king, he said, but he
suspected his courtiers. John of Salisbury had cautioned
him, and the pope had cautioned him, against so indecent a
requisition. Lewis said it was unreasonable. Becket said
then that he must have the kiss of peace as a sign that the
king was really reconciled to him. He probably knew that
the kiss would and must be withheld from him until he had
given proofs that he meant in earnest to carry out his engagements. The king said coldly that he did not mean, and
had never meant, to injure the Church. He was willing to
leave the whole question between himself and the archbishop
either to the peers and prelates of France or to the French
universities. More he could not do. The conference at
Montmartre ended, as Becket meant that it should end, in
nothing.

He sent off dispatches to the Archbishop of Sens and to
his Roman agents, entirely well satisfied with himself, and
bidding them tell the pope that Normandy had only to be
laid under interdict, and that the field was won. Once
more he had painfully to discover that he had been building
on a quicksand. Instead of the interdict, the pope sent

orders to the Archbishop of Rouen and the Bishop of Nevers to absolve a second time the victims whom he had excommunicated at Clairvaux. Instead of encouragement to go on and smite the king with the spiritual sword, he received a distinct command to abstain for another interval. Last of all, and worst of all, the pope informed him that at the king's request, for certain important purposes, he had granted a commission, as legate over all England, to his rival and enemy the Archbishop of York. The king's envoys had promised that the commission should not be handed to the Archbishop of York till the pope had been again consulted. But the deed was done. The letter had been signed and delivered.[1] The hair shirt and the five daily floggings had been in vain then! Heaven was still inexorable. The archbishop raved like a madman. "Satan was set free for the destruction of the Church." "At Rome it was always the same. Barabbas was let go, and Christ was crucified." "Come what might, he would never submit, but he would trouble the Roman Church no more." [2]

[1] Matthew Paris, *Chronica Majora*, pp. 249, 250.
[2] Becket to Cardinal Albert. Giles, vol. ii. p. 251.

CHAPTER VIII.

BECKET had now been for more than five years in exile. He had fought for victory with a tenacity which would have done him credit had his cause been less preposterous. At length it seemed that hope was finally gone. At the supreme moment another opportunity was thrust into his hands. Henry's health was uncertain; he had once been dangerously ill. The succession to the English crown had not yet settled into fixed routine. Of the Conqueror's sons William had been preferred to Robert. Stephen supplanted Matilda; but the son of Stephen was set aside for Matilda's son. To prevent disputes it had been long decided that Prince Henry must be crowned and receive the homage of the barons while his father was still living.

The pope in person had been invited to perform the ceremony. The pope had found it impossible to go, and among the other inconveniences resulting from Becket's absence the indefinite postponement of this coronation had not been the lightest. The king had been reluctant to invade the acknowledged privilege of the Archbishop of Canterbury, and put it off from year to year. But the country was growing impatient. The archbishop's exile might now be indefinitely protracted. The delay was growing dangerous, and the object of the commission for which the king had asked, and which the pope had granted to the Archbishop of York, was to enable the Archbishop of York to act in the coronation ceremony. The commission in its terms was all that Henry could desire; the pope not only permitted the Archbishop of York to officiate, but enjoined him to do it. Promises were said to have been given that it was not to be used without the pope's consent; but in such a labyrinth of lies little reliance can be placed on statements unconfirmed by writing. The pope did not pretend that he had exacted from the English envoys any written engagement. He had himself signed a paper giving the Archbishop of York the necessary powers, and this paper was in the king's hands.[1] The coronation was the symbol of the struggle in which Becket was now engaged. The sovereign, according to his theory, was the delegate of the Church. In receiving the crown from the hands of the Archbishop of Canterbury, the sovereign formally admitted his dependent position; and so long as it could be maintained that the coronation would not hold unless it was performed either by the Archbishop of Canterbury or by the pope himself, the sovereign's subject state was a practical reality.

Becket saw the favorable moment, and instantly snatched at it. He had many powerful friends in England among the peers and knights. The lay peers, he says in his letters, had always been truer to him than the clergy, they on their part having their own differences with the crown. He had ascertained that the coronation could not be postponed; and if he could make the validity of it to depend on his own presence, he might redeem his past mortifications, and bring Henry to his feet after all. He knew Alexander's nature and set his agents to work upon him. He told them to say that if the coronation was accomplished without his own presence the power of the Roman see in England was gone; and thus, when all seemed lost, he gained the feeble and uncertain pope to his side once more. In keeping with his conduct throughout the whole Becket difficulty, Alexander did not revoke his previous letter. He left it standing as something to appeal to, as an evidence of his goodwill to Henry. But he issued another injunction to

---

[1] Giles, vol. ii. pp. 257, 258. The commission quoted by Giles is evidently the same as that to which the pope referred in his letter to Becket.

the Archbishop of York, strictly forbidding him to officiate;
and he inclosed the injunction to Becket to be used by him
in whatever manner he might think fit. The Archbishop
of York never received this letter. It was given, we are
told, to the Bishop of Worcester, who was in Normandy, and
was on the point of returning to England. The Bishop of
Worcester was detained, and it did not reach its destination.
So runs the story; but the parts will not fit one another,
and there is a mystery left unexplained.[1] This only is
certain, that the inhibition was not served on the Archbishop of York. Rumor may have reached England that
such a thing had been issued; but the commission which had
been formerly granted remained legally unrevoked, and on
the 18th of June Prince Henry was crowned at Westminster in his father's presence by the Archbishop of York
and the Bishops of London, Durham, Rochester, and Salisbury.

It was easy now for Becket to represent to Alexander
that the English bishops had rewarded his kindness to
them by defying his positive injunctions. To the superstitious English barons the existence of the inhibition threw
a doubt on the legality of the coronation, and as men's
minds then were, and with the wild lawless disposition of
such lion cubs as the Plantagenet princes, a tainted title
would too surely mean civil war. By ill-fortune offence
was given at the same time to Lewis, who considered that
his daughter should have been crowned with her husband,
and he resented what he chose to regard as a wilful slight.

---

[1] It would appear from a letter of John of Salisbury that the prohibitory letter had been purposely withheld by Becket, who was allowing
himself to be guided by some idle *vaticinia* or prophecies. John of Salisbury writes to him (Letters, vol. ii. p. 236): "Memineritis quantum peri-
culum et infortunium ad see traxerit mora porrigendi . . . . prohibito-
rias Eboracensi archiepiscopo et episcopis transmarinis. . . . . Subtilitatem
vestram vaticinia quæ non erant a Spiritu deluserunt. . . . . Vaticiniis
ergo renunciemus in posterum, quia nos in hâc parte gravius infortunia
perculerunt."

The pope was told that the coronation oath had been altered, that the liberties of the Church had been omitted, and that the young king had been sworn to maintain the Constitutions of Clarendon. Becket made the most of his opportunity ; mistakes, exaggerations, wilful lies, and culpable credulity did their work effectively; Lewis went to war again, and invaded Normandy ; the pope, believing that he had been tricked and insulted, commanded Henry to make peace with the archbishop under threat of instant personal excommunication of himself and an interdict over his whole dominions. Henry flew back from England to Normandy. In a month he dispelled the illusions of Lewis, and restored peace. It was less easy to calm Alexander, who regarded himself, if not openly defied, yet as betrayed by the breach of the promise that the commission to the Archbishop of York should not be used without a fresh permission from himself. Henry knew that a sentence of excommunication against himself, and an interdict over his French dominions, was seriously possible. The risk was too great to be incurred without another effort to compose the weary quarrel. The archbishop, too, on his side had been taught by often repeated experience that the pope was a broken reed. Many times the battle seemed to have been won, and the pope's weakness or ill-will had snatched the victory from him. He had left England because he thought the continent a more promising field of battle for him. He began to think that final success, if he was ever to obtain it, would only be possible to him in his own see, among his own people, surrounded by his powerful friends. He too, on his side, was ready for a form of agreement which would allow him to return and repossess himself of the large revenues of which he had felt the want so terribly. More than once he and Henry met and separated without a conclusion. At length at Frêteval in Vendôme, on St. Mary Magdalen's day, July 22, an interview took place in the presence of Lewis and a vast assemblage of prelates and knights and nobles ; where, on the terms which had been arranged at Montmartre, the king and the archbishop consented to be reconciled. The kiss which before had been the difficulty was not offered by Henry and was not demanded by Becket ; but according to the account given by Herbert, who describes what he himself witnessed, and relates what Becket told him, after the main points were settled, the king and the archbishop rode apart out of hearing of every one but themselves. There the archbishop asked the king whether he might censure the bishops who had officiated at the coronation. The king, so the archbishop informed his friends, gave his full and free consent. The archbishop sprang from his horse in gratitude to the king's feet. The king alighted as hastily, and held the archbishop's stirrup as he remounted. These gestures the spectators saw and wondered at, unable, as Herbert says, to conjecture what was passing till it was afterwards explained to them.

That the king should have consented as absolutely and unconditionally as Becket said that he did, or even that he should have consented at all in Becket's sense of the word, to the excommunication of persons who had acted by his own orders and under a supposed authority from the pope, is so unlikely in itself, so inconsistent with Henry's conduct afterwards, that we may feel assured that Henry's account of what took place would, if we knew it, have been singularly different. But we are met with a further difficulty. Herbert says positively that the conversation between Becket and the king was private between themselves, that no one heard it or knew the subject of it except from Becket's report. Count Theobald of Blois asserted, in a letter to the pope, that in his presence (*me præsente*) the archbishop complained of the conduct of the English prelates, and that the king empowered him to pass sentence on them. Yet more remarkably, the archbishop afterwards at Canterbury insisted to Reginald Fitzurse that the king's

6

promises to him had been given in the audience of 500 peers, knights, and prelates, and that Sir Reginald himself was among the audience. Fitzurse denied that he heard the king give any sanction to the ·punishment of the bishops. He treated Becket's declaration as absurd and incredible on the face of it. The Count of Blois may have confounded what he himself heard with what Becket told him afterwards, or he may have referred to some other occasion. The charge against the king rests substantially on Becket's own uncorrected word; while, on the other side, are the internal unlikelihood of the permission in itself and the inconsistency of Becket's subsequent action with a belief that he had the king's sanction for what he intended to do. Had he supposed that the king would approve, he would have acted openly and at once. Instead of consulting the king, he had no sooner left the Frêteval conference than he privately obtained from the pope letters of suspension against the Archbishop of York and the Bishop of Durham, and letters of excommunication against the Bishops of London, Salisbury, and Rochester; and while he permitted Henry to believe that he was going home to govern his diocese in peace,[1] he had instruments in his portfolio which were to explode in lightning the moment that he set foot in England, and convulse the country once more.

[1] " Archiepiscopus pacem mecum fecit ad voluntatem meam."

CHAPTER IX.

By the terms of the peace of Frêteval, the archbishop was to be restored to his estates and dignity. He on his part had given assurances of his intentions with which Henry had professed himself satisfied. Private communications had passed between him and the king, the nature of which is only known to us through the archbishop's representations to his friends. That the reconciliation, however, was left incomplete, is evident both from Becket's conduct and from Henry's. The king had made the return of his favor conditional on Becket's conduct. Either he did not trust Becket's promises, or the promises were less ample than he desired.

Immediately after the interview the king became dangerously ill, and for a month he believed that he was dying. Becket returned to Sens, and sent messengers to England to young Henry announcing his approaching return, and requesting that his estates should be made over at once to his own people. The messengers were instructed privately to communicate with his English friends, and ascertain the state of public feeling. The young king named a day on which the trust should be made over to the archbishop's officials, and advised that the archbishop should remain for a while on the continent, and endeavor to recover his father's confidence. The messengers reported that he had many staunch supporters, the Earl of Cornwall among them; but they were unanimously of opinion that it would be unwise for the archbishop to reappear at Canterbury so long as the old king's distrust continued. The peace of Frêteval, therefore, was obviously understood to have been inconclusive by all parties. The inconclusiveness was made still more apparent immediately after.

At the beginning of September, Henry had partially recovered. The archbishop sent John of Salisbury and Herbert of Bosham to him to complain of the delay with the estates. He had been watched, perhaps, more closely than he was aware. The king knew nothing as yet of the intended excommunication of the bishops. But he knew Becket's character. He felt it more than probable that mischief was meditated. He said that he must wait to see how the archbishop conducted himself.

Passionate as usual, the archbishop complained to the pope; he intimated that only his holiness's orders prevented him from revenging his ill-treatment. Prudence, however, told him that if he was to make an effective use of the excommunications which the pope had trusted to him, he must for the present restrain himself. Twice again he saw the king at Tours, and afterwards at Amboise. Henry was reserved, but not unkind. The archbishop had professed a wish for peace. If his behavior after his return to England proved that he was in earnest in these professions — if he remained quietly in his province, and made no further disturbances — the king said that he was prepared to show him every possible kindness.

The king needed no more complete justification of his suspicions than an expression which Becket used in relating this conversation to his friend Herbert. " As the king was speaking," he said, " I thought of the words: ' All these things will I give thee if thou wilt fall down and worship me.' " It is evident on the face of the narrative that the king never gave the conscious sanction to violent measures against the bishops, which Becket pretended afterwards that he had received. In answer to his complaints at Amboise, Henry may have told him that the rights of the see of Canterbury should be assured, and that, if those rights had been impaired, satisfaction should be made to him. To this last conference, and to some such words as these, the Count of Blois may have referred in his letter to the pope. But Becket and his friends put a construction upon the promises which none knew better than they that Henry did not intend. It is as certain that Becket's own professions were no less equivocal — that when he spoke of peace he was thinking only of a peace of which he was to dictate the terms, and that he had already determined to reopen the war on a new stage on the instant of his return to his cathedral.

But the return was now determined on, be the consequences what they might. The English bishops had their friends among the cardinals. In the course of the autumn it became known in England that the archbishop had applied for censures against the bishops, and that the pope had granted them. They advised the king to insist that Becket should bind himself by some more explicit engagements before he should be allowed to land, that he should be examined especially as to whether he had any letters of excommunication from Rome, and that if he were in possession of such letters he should surrender them. Henry preferred to trust to the archbishop's honor, or to the watchfulness of the wardens of the ports. He was weary of the struggle. Doubtless he had his misgivings, as the bishops had; but he had made up his mind that the experiment should be tried, with, on his part at least, a faithful discharge of his own engagements.

The archbishop had gone to Rouen in November to settle accounts with creditors who had advanced him money. He had meant to see Henry once more, but Henry wrote to say that the delay of his return had led to disquieting rumors which ought not to continue. He desired the archbishop to go back to Canterbury at once; and, that he might be subjected to no inconvenience on landing, he sent John of Oxford, whose person was well known, to accompany and protect him. John of Oxford's instructions were, after seeing Becket safe at Canterbury, to go on to the young king and give orders for the immediate restoration of the property of the see.

The die was cast. The archbishop resolved to go. There was abundant disaffection in England. In the spring of this very year the king had been obliged to suspend the sheriffs in every county, and ultimately to remove many of them, for extortion and oppression.[1] The clergy were lukewarm in his interests; but there were better reasons for relying upon the nobles. The king had thrust a bridle in their mouths, restraining what they called their liberties, and many of them, as was afterwards proved, were ready to make common cause with the Church against the Crown. The archbishop was perfectly right in expecting to find among the laity a party who would stand by him. He went once more to Sens to take leave of his entertainers. After an affectionate parting with Lewis and the Queen of France, retaining still his old taste for magnificence, he rode down to the coast with an escort of a hundred cavaliers, and there once more, separated from him but by a few hours' sail, lay the white cliffs of England.

It was thought likely, if it was not known for certain, that Becket would bring with him letters from the pope, and the introduction of such letters, if to the hurt of any English subject, was against the law, without a written license from the king. The duty of the wardens of the ports was to search the persons and the baggage of any one whom there was ground for suspecting, and on reaching the coast Becket learned that the three prelates who were to be excommunicated, the Sheriff of Kent, Sir Ranulf de Broc, and Sir Reginald de Warenne, one of the council of the young king, were waiting for him at Dover to ascertain whether he was the bearer of any such explosive missile. The future martyr was not select in his language. " Arch-devils," "priests of Baal," " standard-bearers of the Balaam-

[1] Benedict.

ites," "children of perdition," were the common phrases
with which he described the unfortunate bishops who were
thus trying to escape their sentences. To outwit their vigi-
lance, a day or two before he meant to sail, he sent over a
boy in a small vessel whose insignificant appearance would
attract no attention. The boy or nun (for there is reason
to suppose that the bearer was a woman disguised) presented himself suddenly before the Archbishop of York in
St. Peter's Oratory at Dover, placed the letter of suspension
in his hands, and disappeared before he had time to learn its
contents. In the same hour, and by the same instrument,
the still more terrible letters of excommunication were
served on the Bishops of London and Salisbury. Their
precautions had been baffled. The shots had been fired
which opened the new campaign, and the mark had been
successfully hit. Sir Ranulf de Broc searched the town
with a drawn sword for the audacious messenger, but the
messenger had vanished.

It would have gone ill with Becket had he landed in the
midst of the storm which the delivery of the letters instantly
kindled. The ground of the censures was the coronation of
the young king. To excommunicate the bishops who had
officiated was to deny the young king's title to the crown.
The archbishop had come back then, it seemed, to defy the
government and light a civil war. The next morning, when
he and his friends were examining the vessel in which they
were about to embark, an English boat ran into the harbor.
Some one leaped on shore, and, coming straight to Herbert,
told him that if the archbishop went to Dover he was a dead
man ; the excommunications had set the country on fire.
A rapid council was held. Several of the priests were
frightened. The certain displeasure of the king was admitted with a frankness which showed how little Becket
really supposed that Henry would approve what he had
done. Becket asked Herbert for advice. Herbert, always
the worst adviser that he could have consulted, said that

they must advance or fall into disgrace. Let the archbishop go boldly forward, and he would tread the dragon under his feet. The worst that could befall him was a glorious martyrdom.

Much of this fine language may have been an afterthought. The archbishop, when a choice of conduct lay before him, was certain to choose the most rash. He decided, however, to avoid Dover, and on the morning of the 1st of December he sailed up the river to Sandwich, with his cross raised conspicuously above the figure-head of his ship. Sandwich was his own town. The inhabitants were lieges of the see, and a vast and delighted crowd was gathered on the quay to receive him. The change of destination was known at Dover Castle. Sir Reginald de Warenne, the Sheriff of Kent, and Ranulf de Broc, had ridden across, and had arrived at Sandwich before the archbishop landed. John of Oxford hurried to them with the king's orders that the archbishop was to be received in peace. They advanced in consequence without their arms, and inquired the meaning of the excommunication of the bishops. To their extreme surprise, they were told that the letters had been issued with the king's knowledge and permission. To so bold an assertion no immediate answer was possible. They pointed to his train, among whom were some French clergy. Strangers coming into England without a passport were required to swear allegiance for the time of their stay. The sheriff said that the priests must take the usual oaths. Becket scornfully answered that no clerk in his company should take any oath at all. He declined further conversation, and bade them come to him after two days to the palace of Canterbury if they had more to say.

Becket passed the remainder of the day at Sandwich. The next morning he set out for his cathedral. Seven years he had been absent, and for all those years his name had been a household word in castle and parsonage, grange and cabin. In England people sympathize instinctively

with every one who opposes the Crown, and between Sandwich and Canterbury Becket was among his own tenants, to
whom he had been a gentler master than Ranulf de Broc.
The short winter day's ride was one long triumphal procession. Old men, women, and children lined the roads on their
knees to beg his blessing. Clergy came at the head of their
parishioners with garlands and banners. Boys chanted
hymns. Slowly at a foot's pace the archbishop made his
way among the delighted multitudes. It was evening before
he reached Canterbury. He went direct to the cathedral.
His face shone as he entered, "like the face of Moses when
he descended from the mount." He seated himself on his
throne, and the monks came one by one and kissed him.
Tears were in all eyes. "My lord," Herbert whispered to
Him, "it matters not now when you depart hence. Christ
has conquered. Christ is now king." "He looked at me."
says Herbert, "but he did not speak."

Strangely in that distant century, where the general history is but outline, and the colors are dim, and the lights
and shadows fall where modern imagination chooses to
throw them, and the great men and women who figured on
the world's stage are, for the most part, only names, the
story of Becket, in these last days of it especially, stands out
as in some indelible photograph, every minutest feature of
it as distinct as if it were present to our eyes. We have the
terrible drama before us in all its details. We see the actors,
we hear their very words, we catch the tones of their voices,
we perceive their motives; we observe them from day to
day, and hour to hour; we comprehend and sympathize
with the passions through the fierce collision of which the
action was worked out to its catastrophe. The importance
of the questions which were at issue, the characters of the
chief performers, and the intense interest with which they
were watched by the spectators, raise the biographies and
letters in which the story is preserved to a level of literary
excellence far beyond what is to be found in all contemporary writings.

The archbishop slept in his desolate palace. No preparations had been made for him. The stores had not been laid in. The barns and byres were empty. Ranulf de Broc had swept up the last harvest, and had left the lands bare. In the morning (December 3) de Warenne and the sheriff reappeared with the chaplains of the three bishops. They had been led to hope, they said, that the archbishop would come home in peace. Instead of peace he had brought a sword. By scattering excommunications without notice, he was introducing confusion into every department of the realm. The very crown was made dependent on the archbishop's will. The law of England was reduced to the archbishop's edicts. Such a assumption could not and would not be allowed. The excommunication of the bishops was a direct blow at the authority of the young king. For the archbishop's own sake they advised him, and in the king's name they commanded him, to take the censures off, or a time might come when he would regret his violence too late to repair it.

Until the issue of the sentences against the three bishops, Alexander had not committed himself to any positive act in Becket's favor, and it had been to compromise the papacy distinctly in the quarrel that the pope's letters had been thus immediately discharged. Becket answered that the excommunications had been issued by the supreme pontiff, and that he could not undo the work of his superior. He admitted, with exasperating satire, that he was not displeased to see his holiness defend the Church with his own hands. To punish men who had broken the law was not to show contempt of the king. He had himself complained to the king of the bishops' conduct, and the king had promised that he should have satisfaction. For the rest he acknowledged no right in the king or any man to challenge his conduct. He bore the spiritual sword, and did not mean to shrink from drawing it against sinners, whatever might be the inconvenience. If the bishops would take an oath to submit to any sentence which the pope might pass upon them, he would strain a point and absolve them; without such an oath, never.

The answer was carried to Dover. Foliot and the Bishop of Salisbury were willing, it was said, to have sworn as Becket prescribed. The archbishop declared that he would spend the last farthing that he possessed rather than yield to such insolence. The young king was at Winchester.[1] De Warenne hastened to him to report Becket's behavior, and probably to ask instructions as to what the bishops should do. They crossed eventually to the old king's court in Normandy, but not till after a delay of more than a fortnight at Dover. Obviously the conduct which they were to pursue was carefully canvassed and deliberately resolved upon. Becket himself, too, found it prudent to offer explanations, and send the Prior of Dover after De Warenne to Winchester to report the archbishop's arrival, and to ask permission for him to present himself. From the rapidity with which events now passed, the prior must have ridden night and day. Young Henry being still under age, the archbishop's messenger was received by his guardians, whom he found in towering indignation. The excommunication was regarded as an invitation to rebellion, and had Henry died in August there undoubtedly would have been rebellion. "Does the archbishop mean to make pagans of us, with his suspensions and curses?" they said; "does he intend to upset the throne?" The prior asked to be allowed to see the young king himself. He assured them that the archbishop had meant no injury to him. No one in the realm besides his father loved the prince more dearly. The displeasure was only that other hands than those of the primate had placed the crown upon his head. He repeated the story that the old king knew what was to be done to the bishops. He trusted that the young king would not refuse to receive a person who only desired to do him loyal service.

[1] Not Woodstock, as is generally said. William of Canterbury, with special reference to localities, says Wintonia.

The court was evidently perplexed by the confident assertions with respect to Henry. The Earl of Cornwall advised that Becket should be allowed to come ; they could hear from himself an explanation of the mystery. Geoffrey Ridel, the Archdeacon of Salisbury, happened, however, to be present. Ridel was one of Henry the Second's most confidential advisers, whom Becket had cursed at Vezelay and habitually spoke of as an archdevil. He had been intimately acquainted with the whole details of the quarrel from its commencement, and was able to affirm positively that things were not as Becket represented. He recommended the guardians to consult the king before the archbishop was admitted ; and the Prior of Dover was, in consequence, dismissed without an answer.

The archbishop had committed himself so deeply that he could not afford to wait. His hope was to carry the country with him before the king could interfere, or at least to have formed a party too strong to be roughly dealt with. The Prior of Dover not having brought back a positive prohibition, he left Canterbury professedly to go himself to Winchester : but he chose to take London in his way ; it was easy to say that he had been long absent ; that his flock required his presence ; that there were children to be confirmed, candidates for the priesthood to be ordained — holy rites of all kinds, too long neglected, to be attended to. There was no difficulty in finding an excuse for a circuit through the province ; and the archiepiscopal visitation assumed the form of a military parade. Few as the days had been since he had set his foot on the English shore, he had contrived to gather about him a knot of laymen of high birth and station. *Quidam illustres*, certain persons of distinction, attended him with their armed retainers, and, surrounded by a steel-clad retinue with glancing morions and bristling lances, the archbishop set out for London a week after his return from the Continent. Rochester lay in his way. Rochester Castle was one of the strongholds which he had challenged for his own. The gates of the castle remained closed against him, but the townsmen received him as their liege lord. As he approached Southwark the citizens poured out to greet the illustrious Churchman who had dared to defy his sovereign. A vast procession of three thousand clergy and scholars formed on the road, and went before him chanting a Te Deum; and this passionate display had a deliberate and dangerous meaning which every one who took part in it understood. To the anxious eyes of the court it was a first step in treason, and in the midst of the shouts of the crowd a voice was distinguished, saying, "Archbishop, 'ware the knife!"

It was on December 13 that Becket reached London Bridge. He slept that night close by, at the palace of the old Bishop of Winchester. His movements had been watched. The next morning Sir Jocelyn of Arundel and another knight waited on him with an order from the court at Winchester to return instantly to Canterbury, and to move no more about the realm with armed men. The archbishop had not ventured so far to be frightened at the first hard word. He received Sir Jocelyn as a king might receive a rebel feudatory. With lofty fierceness he said he would go back at no man's bidding if Christmas had not been so near, when he desired to be in his cathedral.[1] "May I not visit my diocese?" he demanded. "Will the king drive off the shepherd that the wolf may tear the flock? Let God see to it!" Arundel said that he had come to deliver the king's commands, not to dispute about them. "Carry back, then, my commands to your king," said the archbishop.[2] "Your commands!" Arundel retorted; "address your commands to those of your own order." Turning sternly to the young lords in the archbishop's suite,

---

[1] "Spiritu fervens respondit se nullatenus propter inhibitionem hanc regressurum, nisi quia tunc jam festus tam solemnis urgebat dies quo ecclesiæ suæ abesse noluit."

[2] "Si et mandata mea regi vestro renunciaturi estis." — William of Canterbury.

he bade them remember their duties, and rode off with his companion.

To obey was to lose the game. Instead of obeying, the archbishop went on to Harrow, a benefice of his own into which an incumbent had been intruded by the Crown. From Harrow he sent for the old Abbot of St. Albans, and dispatched him to Winchester with a list of complaints. At the same time, and to learn the strength of the party at court which he supposed to be ready to stand by him, he sent a monk — apparently William of Canterbury, who tells the story — on a secret and dangerous mission to the Earl of Cornwall. The monk went disguised as a physician, Becket bidding him write word how things were going. The words in which he gave the order show his intention beyond possibility of question. The pretended physician was to go *velut alter Cushy*, and Cushy was the messenger who brought word to David that the Lord had avenged him of his enemies, and that the young king Absalom was dead.[1]

The Earl of Cornwall was well-disposed to Becket, but was true to his king and his country. When the rebellion actually broke out, three years after, the Earl of Cornwall's loyalty saved Henry's crown. He was willing to befriend the archbishop within the limits of law, but not to the extent upon which Becket counted. He received the disguised monk into his household; he examined him closely as to the archbishop's intentions. He would perhaps have allowed him to remain, but a servant of the young king recognized the man through his assumed character as one of Becket's immediate followers, two days after his arrival. The earl bade him begone on the instant, and tell his master to look to himself; his life was in peril.

The Abbot of St. Albans had travelled more slowly The discovery was a bad preparation for his reception. Sir Jocelyn of Arundel had brought back Becket's insolent

[1] 2 Samuel xviii. 31.

answer, and the open disobedience of the order to return to
Canterbury could be construed only as defiance.' To the
alarmed guardians it seemed as if an insurrection might
break out at any moment. The abbot found the court at
Breamore, near Fordingbridge, in Hampshire. He was
admitted, and he presented his schedule of wrongs, which,
after all, was trifling. The archbishop's clergy were forbidden to leave the realm. He had been promised restitution
of his property, but it had been given back to him in ruins.
His game had been destroyed; his woods had been cut
down; his benefices were detained from him. As a last
outrage, since his return Sir Ranulf de Broc had seized a
cargo of wine which he had brought over with the old
king's permission. The vessel in which it had arrived had
been scuttled, and the crew had been incarcerated. God
was injured when his clergy were injured, the abbot said,
and in Becket's name he demanded redress.

The abbot had spoken firmly, but in language and manner he had at least recognized that he was a subject address-
ing his sovereign. A priest in his train, with Becket's own
temper in him, thundered out as the abbot had ended:
" Thus saith the Lord Primate, ' Let man so think of us as
ministers of Christ and stewards of the mysteries of God.
If justice be not done as right demands, ye need not doubt
that we will do our part and use the powers which God has
committed to us.' " The fierce message was delivered
amidst scowling groups of knights and nobles. Hot youths
clenched their fists and clutched their dagger-hilts. A
courtier told the bold priest that, but for the honor of the
king's presence, he should suffer for his insolence. Sir
Reginald de Warenne, who was present, said, " The bows
are bent on both sides." The Earl of Cornwall, fresh from
his conference with Becket's secret messenger, muttered,
" Ere Lent there will be wild work in England."

The archbishop was still at Harrow when the abbot came
back with an account of his reception. Many things the

abbot must have been able to tell him which have been left unrecorded. Thus much, at any rate, must have been made plain — that the archbishop could not count on any immediate armed intervention. For the moment, at least, he would be left to face alone the storm which he had raised. The best that he could now hope to effect would be to bury himself and his enemies in common ruin. He foretold his fate to the abbot, and, resisting entreaties to spend Christmas at St. Albans, went back to Canterbury, where he had still work before him which could be accomplished only in his own cathedral.

CHAPTER X.

THE story now turns to Henry's court in Normandy. Between Southampton and the Norman coast communications were easy and rapid; and the account of the arrival of the censured bishops, with the indignant words which burst from the king at the unwelcome news which he heard from them for the first time, is an imperfect legend in which the transactions of many days must have been epitomized.

The bishops did not leave England till the 20th or 21st of December,[1] and before their appearance the king must have heard already not only of the excommunications and of the daring misuse of his own name, but of the armed progress to London, of the remarkable demonstration there, of the archbishop's defiance of the government, of the mission of the Abbot of St. Albans, of the threats of the priest, and of the imminent danger of a general rebellion. During the first three weeks of this December many an anxious council must have been held in the Norman court, and many a scheme talked over and rejected for dealing with this impracticable firebrand. What could be done with him? No remedy was now available but a violent one. The law could not restrain a man who claimed to be superior to law and whose claims the nation was not prepared directly to deny. Three centuries later the solution would have been a formal trial, with the block and axe as the sequel of a judicial sentence. Ecclesiastical pretensions were still formidable under Tudors, but the State had acquired strength

---

[1] Herbert says that they arrived at Bayeux *paucis diebus ante natalem Domini.*

7

to control them. In our own day the phantom has been exorcised altogether, and an archbishop who used Becket's language would be consigned to an asylum. In Becket's own time neither of these methods was possible. Becket himself could neither be borne with, consistently with the existence of the civil government, nor resisted save at the risk of censures which even the king scarcely dared to encounter. A bishop might have committed the seven deadly sins, but his word was still a spell which could close the gates of heaven. The allegiance of the people could not be depended upon for a day if Becket chose to declare the king excommunicated, unless the pope should interfere; and the pope was an inadequate resource in a struggle for the supremacy of the Church over the State. It was not until secular governments could look popes and bishops in the face, and bid them curse till they were tired, that the relations of Church and State admitted of legal definition. Till that time should arrive the ecclesiastical theory was only made tolerable by submitting to the checks of tacit compromise and practical good sense.

Necessities for compromises of this kind exist at all times. In the most finished constitutions powers are assigned to the different branches of the State which it would be inconvenient or impossible to remove, yet which would cause an immediate catastrophe if the theory were made the measure of practice. The Crown retains a prerogative at present which would be fatal to it if strained. Parliament would make itself intolerable if it asserted the entire privileges which it legally possesses. The clergy in the twelfth century were allowed and believed to be ministers of God in a sense in which neither Crown nor baron dared appropriate the name to themselves. None the less the clergy could not be allowed to reduce Crown and barons into entire submission to themselves. If either churchman or king broke the tacit bargain of mutual moderation which enabled them to work together harmoniously, the relations between the two orders might not admit of more satisfactory theoretic adjustment; but there remained the resource to put out of the way the disturber of the peace.

Fuel ready to kindle was lying dry throughout Henry's dominions. If Becket was to be allowed to scatter excommunications at his own pleasure, to travel through the country attended by knights in arms, and surrounded by adoring fools who regarded him as a supernatural being, it was easy to foresee the immediate future of England and of half France. To persons, too, who knew the archbishop as well as Henry's court knew him, the character of the man himself who was causing so much anxiety must have been peculiarly irritating. Had Becket been an Anselm, he might have been credited with a desire to promote the interests of the Church, not for power's sake, but for the sake of those spiritual and moral influences which the Catholic Church was still able to exert, at least in some happy instances. But no such high ambition was to be traced either in Becket's agitation or in Becket's own disposition. He was still the self-willed, violent, unscrupulous chancellor, with the dress of the saint upon him, but not the nature. His cause was not the mission of the Church to purify and elevate mankind, but the privilege of the Church to control the civil government, and to dictate the law in virtue of magical powers which we now know to have been a dream and a delusion. His personal religion was not the religion of a regenerated heart, but a religion of self-torturing asceticism, a religion of the scourge and the hair shirt, a religion in which the evidences of grace were to be traced not in humbleness and truth, but in the worms and maggots which crawled about his body. He was the impersonation, not of what was highest and best in the Catholic Church, but of what was falsest and worst. The fear which he inspired was not the reverence willingly offered to a superior nature, but a superstitious terror like that felt for witches and enchanters, which brave men at the call of a higher duty could dare to defy.

No one knows what passed at Bayeux during the first weeks of that December. King and council, knights and nobles, squires and valets must' have talked of little else but Becket and his doings. The pages at Winchester laid their hands on their dagger-hilts when the priest delivered his haughty message. The peers and gentlemen who surrounded Henry at Bayeux are not likely to have felt more gently as each day brought news from England of some fresh audacity. At length a few days before Christmas, the three bishops arrived. Two were under the curse, and could not be admitted into the king's presence. The Archbishop of York, being only suspended, carried less contamination with him. At a council the archbishop was introduced, and produced Alexander's letters. From these it appeared not only that he and the other bishops were denounced by name, but that every person who had taken any part in the young king's coronation was by implication excommunicated also. It is to be remembered that the king had received a positive sanction for the coronation from Alexander; that neither he nor the bishops had received the prohibition till the ceremony was over; and that the prohibitory letter, which it is at least possible that the king would have respected, had been kept back by Becket himself.

The Archbishop of York still advised forbearance, and an appeal once more to Rome. The pope would see at last what Becket really was, and would relieve the country of him. But an appeal to Rome would take time, and England meanwhile might be in flames. "By God's eyes," said the king, "if all are excommunicated who were concerned in the coronation, I am excommunicated also." Some one (the name of the speaker is not mentioned) said that there would be no peace while Becket lived. With the fierce impatience of a man baffled by a problem which he has done his best to solve, and has failed through no fault of his own, Henry is reported to have exclaimed: "Is this varlet that I loaded with kindness, that came first to court to me on a lame mule, to insult me and my children, and take my crown from me? What cowards have I about me, that no one will deliver me from this lowborn priest!" It is very likely that Henry used such words. The greatest prince that ever sat on throne, if tried as Henry had been, would have said the same; and Henry had used almost the same language to the bishops at Chinon in 1166. But it is evident that much is still untold. These passionate denunciations can be no more than the outcome of long and ineffectual deliberation. Projects must have been talked over and rejected; orders were certainly conceived which were to be sent to the archbishop, and measures were devised for dealing with him short of his death. He was to be required to absolve the censured bishops. If he refused, he might be sent in custody to the young king, he might be brought to Normandy, he might be exiled from the English dominions, or he might be imprisoned in some English castle. Indications can be traced of all these plans; and something of the kind would probably have been resolved upon, although it must have been painfully clear also that, without the pope's help, none of them would really meet the difficulty. But the result was that the knights about the court, seeing the king's perplexity, determined to take the risk on themselves, and deliver both him and their country. If the king acted, the king might be excommunicated, and the empire might be laid under interdict, with the consequences which every one foresaw. For their own acts the penalty would but fall upon themselves. They did not know, perhaps, distinctly what they meant to do, but something might have to be done which the king must condemn if they proposed it to him.

> But being done unknown,
> He would have found it afterwards well done.

Impetuous loyalty to the sovereign was in the spirit of the age.

Among the gentlemen about his person whom Henry had intended to employ, could he have resolved upon the instructions which were to be given to them, were four knights of high birth and large estate — Sir Reginald Fitzurse, of Somersetshire, a tenant in chief of the Crown, whom Becket himself had originally introduced into the court; Sir Hugh de Morville, custodian of Knaresborough Castle, and justiciary of Northumberland ; Sir William de Tracy, half a Saxon, with royal blood in him ; and Sir Richard le Breton, who had been moved to volunteer in the service by another instance of Becket's dangerous meddling.   Le Breton was a friend of the king's brother William, whom the archbishop had separated from the lady to whom he was about to be married, on some plea of consanguinity.   Sir William de Mandeville and others were to have been joined in the commission.   But these four chose to anticipate both their companions and their final orders, and started alone.[1] Their disappearance was observed.   An express was sent to recall them, and the king supposed that they had returned.   But they had gone by separate routes to separate ports.   The weather was fair for the season of the year, with an east wind perhaps ; and each had found a vessel without difficulty to carry him across the Channel.   The rendezvous was Sir Ranulf de Broc's castle of Saltwood, near Hythe, thirteen miles from Canterbury.

The archbishop meanwhile had returned from his adventurous expedition.   The young king and his advisers had determined to leave him no fair cause of complaint, and had sent orders for the restoration of his wine and the release of the captured seamen ; but the archbishop would not wait

---

[1] Mandeville came afterwards to Canterbury, and being asked what he had been prepared to do if he had found the archbishop alive, he said "that he would have taken the archbishop sharply to task for his attacks upon his sovereign : if the archbishop had been reasonable, there would have been peace; if he had persisted in his obstinacy and presumption, beyond doubt he would have been compelled to yield." Mandeville, indisputably, had direct instructions from the king. — *Materials*, vol. i. p. 126.

for the State to do him justice. On Christmas Eve he was
further exasperated by the appearance at the gate of his
palace of one of his sumpter mules, which had been brutally
mutilated by Sir Ranulf de Broc's kinsman Robert. "The
viper's brood," as Herbert de Bosham said, "were lifting up
their heads. The hornets were out. Bulls of Bashan com-
passed the archbishop round about." The Earl of Cornwall's warning had reached him, but "fight, not flight," was
alone in his thoughts. He, too, was probably weary of the
strife, and may have felt that he would serve his cause
more effectually by death than by life. On Christmas day
he preached in the cathedral on the text "Peace to men of
good will." There was no peace, he said, except to men
of good will. He spoke passionately of the trials of the
Church. As he drew towards an end he alluded to the possibility of his own martyrdom. He could scarcely articu-
late for tears. The congregation were sobbing round him.
Suddenly his face altered, his tone changed. Glowing with
anger, with the fatal candles in front of him, and in a voice
of thunder, the solemn and the absurd strangely blended in
the overwhelming sense of his own wrongs, he cursed the
intruders into his churches; he cursed Sir Ranulf de Broc;
he cursed Robert de Broc for cutting off his mule's tail;
he cursed by name several of the old king's most intimate
councillors who were at the court in Normandy. At each
fierce imprecation he quenched a light, and dashed down
a candle. "As he spoke," says the enthusiastic Herbert,
"you saw the very beast of the prophet's vision, with the
face of a lion and the face of a man." He had drawn the
spiritual sword, as he had sworn that he would. So expe-
rienced a man of the world could not have failed to foresee
that he was provoking passions which would no longer
respect his office, and that no rising in England would
now be in time to save him. He was in better spirits, it
was observed, after he had discharged his anathema. The
Christmas festival was held in the hall. Asceticism was a

virtue which was never easy to him. He indulged his natural inclinations at all permitted times, and on this occasion he ate and drank more copiously than usual.

The next day Becket received another warning that he was in personal danger. He needed no friends to tell him that. The only attention which he paid to these messages was to send his secretary Herbert and his crossbearer Alexander Llewellyn to France, to report his situation to Lewis and to the Archbishop of Sens.[1] He told Herbert at parting that he would see his face no more.

So passed at Canterbury Saturday, Sunday, and Monday, the 26th, 27th, and 28th of December. On that same Monday afternoon the four knights arrived at Saltwood. They were expected, for Sir Ranulf with a party of men-at-arms had gone to meet them. There on their arrival they learned the fresh excommunications which had been pronounced against their host and against their friends at the court. The news could only have confirmed whatever resolutions they had formed.

On the morning of the 29th they rode with an escort of horse along the old Roman road to Canterbury. They halted at St. Augustine's Monastery, where they were entertained by the abbot elect, Becket's old enemy, the scandalous Clarembald. They perhaps dined there. At any rate they issued a proclamation bidding the inhabitants remain quiet in their houses, in the king's name, and then, with some of Clarembald's armed servants in addition to their own party, they went on to the great gate of the archbishop's palace. Leaving their men outside, the four knights alighted and entered the court. They unbuckled their swords, leaving them at the lodge, and, throwing gowns over their armor, they strode across to the door of the hall. Their appearance could hardly have been unexpected.

---

[1] One of his complaints, presented by the Abbot of St. Albans, had been that his clergy were not allowed to leave the realm. There seems to have been no practical difficulty.

It was now between three and four o'clock in the afternoon. They had been some time in the town, and their arrival could not fail to have been reported. The archbishop's midday meal was over. The servants were dining on the remains, and the usual company of mendicants were waiting for their turn. The archbishop had been again disturbed at daybreak by intimation of danger. He had advised any of his clergy who were afraid to escape to Sandwich ; but none of them had left him. He had heard mass as usual. He had received his customary floggings. At dinner he had drunk freely, observing, when some one remarked upon it, that he that had blood to lose needed wine to support him. Afterwards he had retired into an inner room with John of Salisbury, his chaplain Fitzstephen, Edward Grim of Cambridge, who was on a visit to him, and several others, and was now sitting in conversation with them in the declining light of the winter afternoon till the bell should ring for vespers.

The knights were recognized, when they entered the hall, as belonging to the king's court. The steward invited them to eat. They declined, and desired him to inform the archbishop that they had arrived with a message from the Court. This was the first communication which the archbishop had received from Henry since he had used his name so freely to cover acts which, could Henry have anticipated them, would have barred his return to Canterbury forever. The insincere professions of peace had covered an intention of provoking a rebellion. The truth was now plain. There was no room any more for excuse or palliation. What course had the king determined on ?

The knights were introduced. They advanced. The archbishop neither spoke nor looked at them, but continued talking to a monk who was next him. He himself was sitting on a bed. The rest of the party present were on the floor. The knights seated themselves in the same manner, and for a few moments there was silence. Then Becket's

black, restless eye glanced from one to the other. He
slightly noticed Tracy; and Fitzurse said a few unrecorded
sentences to him, which ended with "God help you!" To
Becket's friends the words sounded like insolence. They
may have meant no more than pity for the deliberate fool
who was forcing destruction upon himself.

Becket's face flushed. Fitzurse went on: "We bring
you the commands of the king beyond the sea; will you
hear us in public or in private?" Becket said he cared not.
"In private, then," said Fitzurse. The monks thought
afterwards that Fitzurse had meant to kill the archbishop
where he sat. If the knights had entered the palace,
thronged as it was with men, with any such intention, they
would scarcely have left their swords behind them. The
room was cleared, and a short altercation followed, of which
nothing is known save that it ended speedily in high words
on both sides. Becket called in his clergy again, his lay
servants being excluded,[1] and bade Fitzurse go on. "Be it
so," Sir Reginald said. "Listen then to what the king says.
When the peace was made, he put aside all his complaints
against you. He allowed you to return, as you desired,
free to your see. You have now added contempt to your
other offences. You have broken the treaty. You have
allowed your pride to tempt you to defy your lord and master to your own sorrow. You have censured the bishops
by whose administration the prince was crowned. You
have pronounced an anathema against the king's ministers,
by whose advice he is guided in the management of the
Empire. You have made it plain that if you could you
would take the prince's crown from him. Your plots and
contrivances to attain your ends are notorious to all men.
Say, then, will you attend us to the king's presence, and
there answer for yourself? For this we are sent."

The archbishop declared that he had never wished any
hurt to the prince. The king had no occasion to be dis-

---

[1] "Laicis omnibus exclusis."

pleased if crowds came about him in the towns and cities after having been so long deprived of his presence. If he had done any wrong he would make satisfaction, but he protested against being suspected of intentions which had never entered his mind.

Fitzurse did not enter into an altercation with him, but continued : "The king commands further that you and your clerks repair without delay to the young king's presence, and swear allegiance, and promise to amend your faults."

The archbishop's temper was fast rising. " I will do whatever may be reasonable," he said, " but I tell you plainly the king shall have no oaths from me, nor from any one of my clergy. There has been too much perjury already. I have absolved many, with God's help, who had perjured themselves.[1] I will absolve the rest when He permits.

" I understand you to say that you will not obey," said Fitzurse; and went on in the same tone : " The king commands you to absolve the bishops whom you have excommunicated without his permission (*absque licentiâ suâ*)."

" The pope sentenced the bishops," the archbishop said. " If you are not pleased, you must go to him. The affair is none of mine."

Fitzurse said it had been done at his instigation, which he did not deny; but he proceeded to reassert that the king had given him permission. He had complained at the time of the peace of the injury which he had suffered in the coronation, and the king had told him that he might obtain from the pope any satisfaction for which he liked to ask.

If this was all the consent which the king had given, the pretence of his authority was inexcusable. Fitzurse could scarce hear the archbishop out with patience. " Ay, ay ! " said he; " will you make the king out to be a traitor, then ? The king gave you leave to excommunicate the bishops

---

[1] He was alluding to the bishops who had sworn to the Constitutions of Clarendon.

when they were acting by his own order! It is more than we can bear to listen to such monstrous accusations."

John of Salisbury tried to check the archbishop's imprudent tongue, and whispered to him to speak to the knights in private: but when the passion was on him, no mule was more ungovernable than Becket. Drawing to a conclusion, Fitzurse said to him: "Since you refuse to do any one of those things which the king requires of you, his final commands are that you and your clergy shall forthwith depart out of this realm and out of his dominions, never more to return.[1] You have broken the peace and the king cannot trust you again."

Becket answered wildly that he would not go — never again would he leave England. Nothing but death should now part him from his church. Stung by the reproach of ill-faith, he poured out the catalogue of his own injuries. He had been promised restoration, and instead of restoration he had been robbed and insulted. Ranulf de Broc had laid an embargo on his wine. Robert de Broc had cut off his mule's tail, and now the knights had come to menace him.

De Morville said that if he had suffered any wrong he had only to appeal to the council, and justice would be done.

Becket did not wish for the council's justice. "I have complained enough," he said; "so many wrongs are daily heaped upon me that I could not find messengers to carry the tale of them. I am refused access to the court. Neither one king nor the other will do me right. I will endure it no more. I will use my own powers as archbishop, and no child of man shall prevent me."

---

[1] "Hoc est præceptum regis, ut de regno et terrâ quæ ipsius subjacet imperio cum tuis omnibus egrediaris; neque enim pax erit tibi vel tuorum cuiquam ab hâc die, quia pacem violâsti." These remarkable words are given by Grim, who heard them spoken. After the deliberate fraud of which Becket had been guilty towards the pope in suppressing the inhibitory letter addressed to the Archbishop of York, Alexander might perhaps have been induced at last to approve of such a measure.

"You will lay the realm under interdict, then, and ex-communicate the whole of us?" said Fitzurse.

"So God help me," said one of the others, "he shall not do that. He has excommunicated over-many already. We have borne too long with him."

The knights sprang to their feet, twisting their gloves and swinging their arms. The archbishop rose. In the general noise words could no longer be accurately heard. At length the knights moved to leave the room, and, ad-dressing the archbishop's attendants, said, "In the king's name we command you to see that this man does not escape."

"Do you think I shall fly, then?" cried the archbishop. "Neither for the king nor for any living man will I fly. You cannot be more ready to kill me than I am to die. . . . Here you will find me," he shouted, following them to the door as they went out, and calling after them. Some of his friends thought that he had asked De Morville to come back and speak quietly with him, but it was not so. He returned to his seat still excited and complaining.

"My lord," said John of Salisbury to him, "it is strange that you will never be advised. What occasion was there for you to go after these men and exasperate them with your bitter speeches? You would have done better surely by being quiet and giving them a milder answer. They mean no good, and you only commit yourself."

The archbishop sighed, and said, "I have done with ad-vice. I know what I have before me."

It was four o'clock when the knights entered. It was now nearly five; and unless there were lights the room must have been almost dark. Beyond the archbishop's chamber was an ante-room, beyond the ante-room the hall. The knights, passing through the hall into the quadrangle, and thence to the lodge, called their men to arms. The great gate was closed. A mounted guard was stationed outside with orders to allow no one to go out or in. The knights threw off their cloaks and buckled on their swords. This was the work of a few minutes. From the cathedral tower the vesper bell was beginning to sound. The archbishop had seated himself to recover from the agitation of the preceding scene, when a breathless monk rushed in to say that the knights were arming. "Who cares? Let them arm," was all that the archbishop said. His clergy were less indifferent. If the archbishop was ready for death they were not. The door from the hall into the court was closed and barred, and a short respite was thus secured. The intention of the knights, it may be presumed, was to seize the archbishop and carry him off to Saltwood, or to De Morville's castle at Knaresborough, or perhaps to Normandy. Coming back to execute their purpose, they found themselves stopped by the hall door. To burst it open would require time ; the ante-room between the hall and the archbishop's apartments opened by an oriel window and an outside stair into a garden. Robert de Broc, who knew the house well, led the way to it in the dark. The steps were broken, but a ladder was standing against the window, by which the knights mounted, and the crash of the falling casement told the fluttered group about the archbishop that their enemies were upon them. There was still a moment. The party who entered by the window, instead of turning into the archbishop's room, first went into the hall to open the door and admit their comrades. From the archbishop's room a second passage, little used, opened into the northwest corner of the cloister, and from the cloister there was a way into the north transept of the cathedral. The cry was, "To the church. To the church." There at least there would be immediate safety.

The archbishop had told the knights that they would find him where they left him. He did not choose to show fear, or he was afraid, as some thought, of losing his martyrdom. He would not move. The bell had ceased. They reminded him that vespers had begun, and that he ought to be in the cathedral. Half yielding, half resisting, his friends swept him down the passage into the cloister. His cross had been forgotten in the haste. He refused to stir till it was fetched and carried before him as usual. Then only, himself incapable of fear, and rebuking the terror of the rest, he advanced deliberately to the door into the south transept.[1] His train was scattered behind him, all along the cloister from the passage leading out of the palace. As he entered the church cries were heard from which it became plain that the knights had broken into the archbishop's room, had found the passage, and were following him. Almost immediately Fitzurse, Tracy, De Morville, and Le Breton were discerned, in the dim light, coming through the cloister in their armor, with drawn swords, and axes in their left hands. A company of men-at-arms was behind them. In front they were driving before them a frightened flock of monks.

From the middle of the transept in which the archbishop was standing a single pillar rose into the roof. On the eastern side of it opened a chapel of St. Benedict, in which were the tombs of several of the old primates. On the west, running, of course, parallel to the nave, was a lady chapel. Behind the pillar steps led up into the choir, where voices were already singing vespers. A faint light may have been reflected into the transept from the choir tapers, and candles may perhaps have been burning before the altars in the two chapels — of light from without through the windows at that hour there could have been none. Seeing the knights coming on, the clergy who had entered with the archbishop closed the door and barred it. " What do

---

[1] Those who desire a more particular account of the scene about to be described should refer to Dean Stanley's essay on the murder of Becket, which is printed in his *Antiquities of Canterbury*. Along with an exact knowledge of the localities and a minute acquaintance with the contemporary narratives, Dr. Stanley combines the far more rare power of historical imagination, which enables him to replace out of his materials an exact picture of what took place.

you fear?" he cried in a clear, loud voice. "Out of the way, you cowards! The Church of God must not be made a fortress." He stepped back and reopened the door with his own hands, to let in the trembling wretches who had been shut out among the wolves. They rushed past him, and scattered in the hiding-places of the vast sanctury, in the crypt, in the galleries, or behind the tombs. All, or almost all, even of his closest friends, William of Canterbury, Benedict, John of Salisbury himself forsook him to shift for themselves, admitting frankly that they were unworthy of martyrdom. The archbishop was left alone with his chaplain Fitzstephen, Robert of Merton his old master, and Edward Grim, the stranger from Cambridge — or perhaps with Grim only, who says that he was the only one who stayed, and was the only one certainly who showed any sign of courage. A cry had been raised in the choir that armed men were breaking into the cathedral. The vespers ceased; the few monks assembled left their seats and rushed to the edge of the transept, looking wildly into the darkness.

The archbishop was on the fourth step beyond the central pillar ascending into the choir when the knights came in. The outline of his figure may have been just visible to them, if light fell upon it from candles in the lady chapel. Fitzurse passed to the right of the pillar, De Morville, Tracy, and Le Breton to the left. Robert de Broc and Hugh Mauclerc, another apostate priest, remained at the door by which they entered. A voice cried, "Where is the traitor? Where is Thomas Becket?" There was silence; such a name could not be acknowledged. "Where is the archbishop?" Fitzurse shouted. "I am here," the archbishop replied, descending the steps, and meeting the knights full in the face. "What do you want with me? I am not afraid of your swords. I will not do what is unjust." The knights closed round him. "Absolve the persons whom you have excommunicated," they said, "and take off the suspensions." "They have made no satisfaction," he answered; "I will not." "Then you shall die as you have deserved," they said.

They had not meant to kill him — certainly not at that time and in that place. One of them touched him on the shoulder with the flat of his sword, and hissed in his ears, "Fly, or you are a dead man." There was still time; with a few steps he would have been lost in the gloom of the cathedral, and could have concealed him in any one of a hundred hiding-places. But he was careless of life, and he felt that his time was come. "I am ready to die," he said. "May the Church through my blood obtain peace and liberty! I charge you in the name of God that you hurt no one here but me. The people from the town were now pouring into the cathedral; De Morville was keeping them back with difficulty at the head of the steps from the choir, and there was danger of a rescue. Fitzurse seized him, meaning to drag him off as a prisoner. He had been calm so far; his pride rose at the indignity of an arrest. "Touch me not, thou abominable wretch!" he said, wrenching his cloak out of Fitzurse's grasp. "Off, thou pander, thou!"[1] Le Breton and Fitzurse grasped him again, and tried to force him upon Tracy's back. He grappled with Tracy and flung him to the ground, and then stood with his back against the pillar, Edward Grim supporting him. Fitzurse, stung by the foul epithet which Becket had thrown at him, swept his sword over him and dashed off his cap. Tracy, rising from the pavement, struck direct at his head. Grim raised his arm and caught the blow. The arm fell broken, and the one friend found faithful sank back disabled against the wall. The sword, with its remaining force, wounded the archbishop above the forehead, and the blood trickled down his face. Standing firmly, with his hands clasped, he bent his neck for the death-stroke, saying in a low voice, "I am prepared to die for Christ and for His Church."

[1] "Lenonem appellans." In extreme moments Becket was never able to maintain his dignity.

8

These were his last words. Tracy again struck him. He fell forward upon his knees and hands. In that position Le Breton dealt him a blow which severed the scalp from the head and broke the sword against the stone, saying, "Take that for my Lord William." De Broc or Mauclerc — the needless ferocity was attributed to both of them — strode forward from the cloister door, set his foot on the neck of the dead lion, and spread the brains upon the pavement with his sword's point. "We may go," he said; "the traitor is dead, and will trouble us no more."

Such was the murder of Becket, the echoes of which are still heard across seven centuries of time, and which, be the final judgment upon it what it may, has its place among the most enduring incidents of English history. Was Becket a martyr, or was he justly executed as a traitor to his sovereign? Even in that supreme moment of terror and wonder, opinions were divided among his own monks. That very night Grim heard one of them say, "He is no martyr, he is justly served." Another said, scarcely feeling, perhaps, the meaning of the words, "He wished to be king and more than king. Let him be king, let him be king." Whether the cause for which he died was to prevail, or whether the sacrifice had been in vain, hung on the answer which would be given to this momentous question. In a few days or weeks an answer came in a form to which in that age no rejoinder was possible, and the only uncertainty which remained at Canterbury was whether it was lawful to use the ordinary prayers for the repose of the dead man's soul, or whether, in consequence of the astounding miracles which were instantly worked by his remains, the pope's judgment ought not to be anticipated, and the archbishop ought not to be at once adored as a saint in heaven.

CHAPTER XI.

MARTYR for the Church of Christ, or turbulent incendiary justly punished for his madness or presumption? That was the alternative which lay before the judgment of the Christian world. On the response which would be given depended interests which stretched far beyond the limits of Becket's own island home. How vast were the issues, how possible was an unfavorable conclusion, may be seen in the passionate language in which Benedict of Canterbury describes the general feeling, and relates the influences by which alone the popular verdict was decided in the archbishop's favor.

Our crowned head was taken from us, the glory of angels and of Angles. We were orphans who had lost their father. The mother Church was desolate, and her children were not lamenting. She sought for some to comfort her, yet found she none. She was weeping, and her children were glad. Our own noble monastery was speechless, and cruel mockers said it was well done. The brethren mingled their bread with tears, but they kept silence. Had not light risen upon us from on high, we had been lost forever. Praised be He who looked upon us in the day of our affliction! All generations shall now call us blessed. When the martyr was slain our young men saw visions, our old men dreamed dreams; and then came the miracles, and we knew that God had exalted the horn of his anointed one.

The sheep were scattered: the hirelings had fled. There had not been found a man who would stand beside the lord of Canterbury against the workers of iniquity. The second part of Christendom had gone astray after the idol Baal, the apostate, the antipope. Who can say what the end might not have been? In the blood of the martyr of Canterbury the Most

High provided an expiation for the sins of the world. The darkness passed away before the splendor of the miracles. The seed of the word sprang up. Unnumbered sinners are converted daily, and beat their breasts and turn back into the fold. Our anointed Gideon had his lamp in a pitcher : the clay of the earthly body was broken, and light shone out. The schismatic Octavian was at once condemned, and Pope Alexander was established in Peter's chair. If Alexander had not been our true father, the martyr who adhered to him would have been defiled by the pitch which he had touched. His miracles prove that he had not been defiled. No man could do such wonders unless God was with him.

And as he died for the Universal Church, so especially he died for the Church of Canterbury. Let his successor not abandon the rights which our holy martyr defended. Let him not despise the law of the Church, or depart from obedience to Pope Alexander. Let his holiness be glad that in these last times, and in the ends of the earth, he has found such a son. Let the children of Canterbury rejoice that the consolation of such miracles has been vouchsafed to them. Let the whole earth exult, and they that dwell therein. On those who walked in darkness the light has shined. The fearful shepherds have learned boldness; the sick are healed; the repenting sinner is forgiven. Through the merits of our blessed martyr the blind see, the lame walk, the lepers are cleansed, the deaf hear, the dead are raised up, the poor have the Gospel preached to them. In him all the miracles of the Gospel are repeated, and find their full completion. Four times the lamps about his tomb have been kindled by invisible hands. An innocent man who was mutilated by the executioner called on the martyr for help and is restored : new eyes and new members have been granted to him. Never anywhere, so soon after death and in so brief a time, has saint been made illustrious by so many and so mighty tokens of God's favor.[1]

Miracles come when they are needed. They come not of fraud, but they come of an impassioned credulity which creates what it is determined to find. Given an enthusiastic desire that God should miraculously manifest Himself, the

[1] *Materials,* vol. ii. p. 21 (abridged).

religious imagination is never long at a loss for facts to prove that He has done so; and in proportion to the magnitude of the interests at stake is the scale of the miraculous interposition. In the eyes of Europe, the cause in which Becket fell was the cause of sacerdotalism as against the prosaic virtues of justice and common sense. Every superstitious mind in Christendom was at work immediately, generating supernatural evidence which should be universal and overwhelming. When once the impression was started that Becket's relics were working miracles, it spread like an epidemic. Either the laws of nature were suspended, or for the four years which followed his death the power and the wish were gone to distinguish truth from falsehood. The most ordinary events were transfigured. That version of any story was held to be the truest which gave most honor to the martyr. That was the falsest which seemed to detract from his glory. As Becket in his life had represented the ambition and arrogance of the Catholic Church, and not its genuine excellence, so it was his fate in death to represent beyond all others the false side of Catholic teaching, and to gather round himself the most amazing agglomerate of lies.

The stream which was so soon to roll in so mighty a volume rose first in the humble breast of Benedict the monk. After the murder the body was lifted by the trembling brotherhood from the spot where it had fallen, and was laid for the night in front of the high altar. The monks then sought their pallets with one thought in the minds of all of them. Was the archbishop a saint, or was he a vain dreamer? God only could decide. Asleep or awake — he was unable to say which — Benedict conceived that he saw the archbishop going towards the altar in his robes, as if to say mass. He approached him trembling. "My lord," he supposed himself to have said, "are you not dead?" The archbishop answered, "I was dead, but I have risen again." "If you are risen, and, as we believe, a martyr," Benedict said, " will you not manifest yourself to the world?" The archbishop showed Benedict a lantern with a candle dimly burning in it. "I bear a light," he said, " but a cloud at present conceals it." He then seemed to ascend the altar steps. The monks in the choir began the introit. The archbishop took the word from them, and in a rich, full voice poured out, "Arise, why sleepest thou, O Lord? Arise, and cast us not forth forever."

Benedict was dreaming; but the dream was converted into instant reality. The word went round the dormitory that the archbishop had risen from the dead and had appeared to Benedict. The monks, scarcely knowing whether they too were awake or entranced, flitted into the cathedral to gaze on the mysterious form before the altar. In the dim winter dawn they imagined they saw the dead man's arm raised as if to bless them. The candles had burnt out. Some one placed new candles in the sockets and lighted them. Those who did not know whose hand had done it concluded that it was an angel's. Contradiction was unheard or unbelieved; at such a moment incredulity was impious. Rumors flew abroad that miracles had already begun, and when the cathedral doors were opened the townspeople flocked in to adore. They rushed to the scene of the murder. They dipped their handkerchiefs in the sacred stream which lay moist upon the stones. A woman whose sight had been weak from some long disease touched her eyes with the blood, and cried aloud that she could again see clearly. Along with the tale of the crime there spread into the country, gathering volume as it rolled, the story of the wonders which had begun; and every pious heart which had beat for the archbishop when he was alive was set bounding with delighted enthusiasm. A lady in Sussex heard of the miracle with the woman. Her sight, too, was failing. *Divinitus inspirata*, under a divine inspiration, which anticipated the judgment of the Church, she prayed to the blessed martyr St. Thomas, and was instantly restored. Two days later a man at Canterbury who was actually blind recovered his sight. The brothers at the cathedral whose faith had been weak were supernaturally strengthened. The last doubter among them was converted by a vision.

In the outside world there were those who said that the miracles were delusion or enchantment; but with the scoffs came tales of the retribution which instantly overtook the scoffers. A priest at Nantes was heard to say that if strange things had happened at Canterbury the cause could not be the merits of the archbishop, for God would not work miracles for a traitor. As "the man of Belial" uttered his blasphemies his eyes dropped from their sockets, and he fell to the ground foaming at the mouth. His companions carried him into a church, replaced the eyeballs, and sprinkled them with holy water, and prayed to St. Thomas for pardon. St. Thomas was slowly appeased, and the priest recovered, to be a sadder and a wiser man.

Sir Thomas of Ecton had known Becket in early youth, and refused to believe that a profligate scoundrel could be a saint.[1] Sir Thomas was seized with a quinsy which almost killed him, and only saved his life by instant repentance.

In vain the De Brocs and their friends attempted to stem the torrent by threatening to drag the body through the streets, to cut it in pieces, and fling it into a cesspool. The mob of Kent would have risen in arms, and burnt their castle over their heads, had they dared to touch so precious a possession. The archbishop was laid in a marble sarcophagus before the altar of St. John the Baptist in the crypt. The brain which De Broc's rude sword had spread out was gathered up by reverent hands, the blood stains were scraped off the stones, and the precious relics were placed on the stone lid where they could be seen by the faithful. When the body was stripped for burial, on the back were seen the

---

[1] "Martyrem libidinosi et nebulonis elogio notans." — William of Canterbury. *Materials*, vol. i.

marks of the stripes which he had received on the morning of his death. The hair shirt and drawers were found swarming (*scaturientes*) with vermin. These transcendent evidences of sanctity were laid beside the other treasures, and a wall was built round the tomb to protect it from profanation, with openings through which the sick and maimed, who now came in daily crowds for the martyr's help, could gaze and be healed.

Now came the more awful question. The new saint was jealous of his honor: was it safe to withold his title from him till the pope had spoken? He had shown himself alive — was it permitted to pray for him as if he were dead? Throughout England the souls of the brethren were exercised by this dangerous uncertainty. In some places the question was settled in the saint's favor by an opportune dream. At Canterbury itself more caution was necessary, and John of Salisbury wrote to the Bishop of Poitiers for advice :

The blind see (he said), the deaf hear, the dumb speak, the lame walk, the devils are cast out. To pray for the soul of one whom God had distinguished by miracles so illustrious is injurious to him, and bears a show of unbelief. We should have sent to consult the pope, but the passages are stopped, and no one can leave the harbors without a passport For ourselves, we have concluded that we ought to recognize the will of God without waiting for the holy father's sanction.[1]

The pope's ultimate resolution it was impossible to doubt. The party of the antipope in England had been put an end to by the miracles. Many people had begun to waver in their allegiance, and now all uncertainty was gone. It was universally admitted that these wonders displayed in favor of a person who had been on Alexander's side conclusively

---

[1] John of Salisbury to the Bishop of Poitiers. Letters, vol. ii. pp. 257, 258 (abridged). How John of Salisbury was able to write both to the Bishop of Poitiers and to the Archbishop of Sens, if he was unable to write to Rome because the passages were stopped, does not appear.

decided the question.[1] Alexander would do well, however, John of Salisbury thought, to pronounce the canonization with as little delay as possible

The epidemic was still in its infancy. The miracles already mentioned had been worked in comparative privacy in the first few weeks which succeeded the martyrdom. Before the summer the archbishop's admirers were contending with each other in every part of Europe which could report the most amazing miracles that had been worked by his intervention or by the use of his name. Pilgrims began to stream to Canterbury with their tales of marvel and their rich thanksgiving offerings. A committee of monks was appointed to examine each story in detail. Their duty was to assure themselves that the alleged miracle was reality and not imagination. Yet thousands were allowed to pass as adequately and clearly proved. Every day under their own eyes the laws of nature were set aside. The aperture in the wall round the tomb contracted or enlarged according to the merit of the visitants. A small and delicate woman could not pass so much as her head through it to look at the relics. She was found to be living in sin. A monster of a man possessed by a devil, but honestly desirous of salvation, plunged through, body and all. The spectators (Benedict among them, who tells the story) supposed it would be necessary to pull the wall down to get him free. He passed out with the same ease with which he had entered. But when the monks told him to repeat the experiment, stone and mortar had resumed their properties.

. The blood gathered on the handkerchiefs from the pavement had shown powers so extraordinary that there was a universal demand for it. The difficulty from the limitation of quantity was got over in various ways. At first it ex-

---

1 "Dubitatur a plurimis an pars domini papæ in quâ stamus de justitiâ niteretur, sed eam a crimine gloriosus martyr absolvit, qui si fautor erat schismatis nequaquam tantis miraculis coruscaret." — To the Archbishop of Sens. Letters, vol. ii. p. 263.

hibited a capacity for self-multiplication. A single drop might be poured into a bottle, and the bottle would be found full. Afterwards a miraculous fountain broke out in the crypt, with the water from which the blood was mixed. The smallest globule of blood, fined down by successive recombinations to a fraction of unimaginable minuteness, imparted to the water the virtues of the perfect original. St. Thomas's water became the favorite remedy for all diseases throughout the Christian world, the sole condition of a cure being that doctor's medicines should be abjured. The behavior of the liquid, as described by Benedict, who relates what he professes to have continually seen, was eccentric and at first incomprehensible. A monk at the fountain distributed it to the pilgrims, who brought wooden boxes in which to carry it away. When poured into these boxes it would sometimes effervesce or boil. More often the box would split in the pilgrim's hand. Some sin unconfessed was supposed to be the cause, and the box itself, after such a misfortune, was left as an offering at the tomb. The splitting action after a time grew less violent, and was confined to a light crack. One day a woman brought a box which became thus slightly injured. The monk to whom she gave it thought it was too good to be wasted, and was meditating in his own mind that he would keep it for himself. At the moment that the wicked thought formed itself the box flew to pieces in his hands with a loud crash. He dropped it, shrieking that it was possessed. Benedict and others ran in, hearing him cry, to find him in an agony of terror. The amusement with which Benedict admits that they listened to his story suggests a suspicion that in this instance at least the incident was not wholly supernatural.[1] Finding boxes liable to these misfortunes, the pilgrims next tried stone bottles, but with no better success — the stone cracked like the wood. A youth at Canterbury suggested tin; the burst-

---

[1] "Hoc miraculum tam joco et risui multis extitit quam admirationi." — *Materials*, vol. ii.

ing miracle ceased, and the meaning of it was then perceived. The pilgrims were intended to carry St. Thomas's water round the world, hung about their necks in bottles which could be at once secure and sufficiently diminutive for transport. A vessel that could be relied on being thus obtained, the trade became enormous. Though the holy thing might not be sold, the recipient of the gift expressed his gratitude by corresponding presents; and no diamond mine ever brought more wealth to its owners than St. Thomas's water brought to the monks of Canterbury.

As time went on the miracles grew more and more prodigious. At first weak eyes were made strong; then sight was restored which was wholly gone. At first sick men were made whole; then dead men were brought back to life. At first there was the unconscious exaggeration of real phenomena; then there was incautious embellishment. Finally, in some instances of course with the best intentions, there was perhaps deliberate lying. To which of these classes the story should be assigned which has now to be told the reader must decide for himself. No miracle in sacred history is apparently better attested. The more complete the evidence, the more the choice is narrowed to the alternative between a real supernatural occurrence and an intentional fraud.

In the year which followed Becket's death there lived near Bedford a small farmer named Aylward. This Aylward, unable to recover otherwise a debt from one of his neighbors, broke into his debtor's house, and took possession of certain small articles of furniture to hold as security. The debtor pursued him, wounded him in a scuffle, and carried him before the head constable of the district, who happened to be Aylward's personal enemy. A charge of burglary was brought against him, with the constable's support. Aylward was taken before the sheriff, Sir Richard Fitzosbert, and committed to Bedford Gaol to await his trial. The gaol chaplain in the interval took charge of his soul, gave him a whip with which to flog himself five times a day, and advised him to consign his cause to the Virgin, and especially to the martyr Thomas. At the end of a month he was brought before the justices at Leighton Buzzard. The constable appeared to prosecute; and his own story not being received as true, he applied for wager of battle with his accuser, or else for the ordeal of hot iron. Through underhand influence the judges refused either of these comparatively favorable alternatives, and sentenced the prisoner to the ordeal of water, which meant death by drowning or else dismemberment. The law of the Conqueror was still in force. The penalty of felony was not the axe or the gallows, but mutilation; and the water ordeal being over, which was merely a form, Aylward, in the presence of a large number of clergy and laity, was delivered to the knife. He bled so much that he was supposed to be dying, and he received the last sacrament. A compassionate neighbor, however, took him into his house, and attended to his wounds, which began slowly to heal. On the tenth night St. Thomas came to his bedside, made a cross on his forehead, and told him that if he presented himself the next day with a candle at the altar of the Virgin in Bedford Church, and did not doubt in his heart, but believed that God was able and willing to cure him, his eyes would be restored. In the morning he related his vision. It was reported to the dean, who himself accompanied him to the altar, the townspeople coming in crowds to witness the promised miracle. The blinded victim of injustice and false evidence believed as he was directed, and prayed as he was directed. The bandages were then removed from the empty eye sockets, and in the hollows two small glittering spots were seen, the size of the eyes of a small bird, with which Aylward pronounced that he could again see. He set off at once to offer his thanks to his preserver at Canterbury. The rumor of the miracle had preceded him, and in London he was detained by the bishop till the truth had been inquired into. The result was a deposition signed by the Mayor and Corporation of Bedford, declaring that they had ascertained the completeness of the mutilation beyond all possibility of doubt.

Very curiously, precisely the same miracle was repeated under similar conditions three years later. Some cavil had perhaps been raised on the sufficiency of the evidence. The burgesses of a country town were not, it may have been thought, men of sufficient knowledge and education to be relied upon in so extraordinary a case. The very ability of a saint to restore parts of the human body which had been removed may have been privately called in question, and to silence incredulity the feat was performed a second time. There appeared in Canterbury in 1176 a youth named Rogers, bringing with him a letter from Hugh, Bishop of Durham, to the prior of the monastery. The letter stated that in the preceding September the bearer had been convicted of theft, and had been mutilated in the usual manner. He had subsequently begged his living in the Durham streets, and was well known to every one in the town to be perfectly blind. In this condition he had prayed to St. Thomas. St. Thomas had appeared to him in a red gown, with a mitre on his head and three wax candles in his hand, and had promised him restoration. From that moment his sight began to return, and in a short time he could discern the smallest objects. Though, as at Bedford, the eyes were *modicæ quantitatis*, exceedingly minute, the functions were perfect. The bishop, to leave no room for mistake, took the oaths of the executioner and the witnesses of the mutilation. The cathedral bells were rung, and thanksgiving services were offered to God and St. Thomas.

So far the Bishop of Durham. But the story received a further confirmation by a coincidence scarcely less singular. When the subject of the miracle came to Canterbury, the judge who had tried him happened to be on a visit to the

monastery. The meeting was purely accidental. The
judge had been interested in the boy, and had closely observed him. He was able to swear that the eyes which he
then saw were not the eyes which had been cut out by the
executioner at Durham, being different from them in form
and color.[1]

When the minds of bishops and judges were thus affected,
we cease to wonder at the thousand similar stories which
passed into popular belief. Many of them are childish,
many grossly ridiculous. The language of the archbishop
on his miraculous appearances was not like his own, but was
the evident creation of the visionary who was the occasion
of his visit ; and his actions were alternately the actions of
a benevolent angel or a malignant imp. But all alike were
received as authentic, and served to swell the flood of illusion which overspread the Christian world. For four years
the entire supernatural administration of the Church econ-
omy was passed over to St. Thomas ; as if Heaven designed
to vindicate the cause of the martyr of Canterbury by
special and extraordinary favor. In vain during those
years were prayers addressed to the Blessed Virgin; in
vain the cripple brought his offerings to shrines where a
miracle had never been refused before. The Virgin and
the other dispensers of divine grace had been suspended
from activity, that the champion of the Church might have
the glory to himself. The elder saints had long gone to
and fro on errands of mercy. They were now allowed to
repose, and St. Thomas was all in all.[2]

---

[1] *Materials*, vol. i. p. 423.

[2] William of Canterbury mentions the case of a man in distress who
prayed without effect to the Virgin. "Hujusmodi prec us," he says,
"sæpius et propensius instabat; similiter et aliorum sanctorum suffragia
postulabat, sed ad invocationem sui nominis non exaudierunt, qui retro
tempora sua glorificationis habuerunt, ut et sua tempora propitiationis
martyr modernus haberet. Pridem cucurrerant quantum potuerunt et
quantum debuerunt signis et prodigiis coruscantes : nunc tandem erat et
novo martyri currendum, ut in catalogo sanctorum mirificus haberetur,

Greater for a time than the Blessed Virgin, greater than the saints!—nay, another superiority was assigned to him still more astounding. The sacrifice of St. Thomas was considered to be wider and more gracious in its operation than the sacrifice on Calvary. Foliot, Bishop of London, so long his great antagonist, was taken ill a few years after the murder, and was thought to be dying. He was speechless. The Bishop of Salisbury sat by him, endeavoring to hear his confession before giving him the sacrament. The voice was choked, the lips were closed; he could neither confess his sins nor swallow his *viaticum*, and nothing lay before him but inevitable hell, when, by a happy thought, sacrament was added to sacrament—the wafer was sprinkled with the water of St. Thomas, and again held to the mouth of the dying prelate. Marvel of marvels! the tightened sinews relaxed. The lips unclosed; the tongue resumed its office; and when all ghostly consolation had been duly offered and duly received, Foliot was allowed to recover.

"O martyr full of mercy!" exclaims the recorder of the miracle, "blessedly forgetful art thou of thy own injuries, who didst thus give to drink to thy disobedient and rebellious brother of the fountain of thy own blood. O deed without example! O act incomparable! Christ gave his flesh and blood to be eaten and drunk by sinners. St. Thomas, who imitated Christ in his passion, imitates Him also in the sacrament. But there is this difference, that Christ damns those who eat and drink Him unworthily, or takes their lives from them, or afflicts them with diseases. The blessed Thomas, doing according to his Master's promise greater things than He, and being more full of mercy than He, gives his blood to his enemies as well as to his friends; and not only does not damn his enemies, but calls

Domino dispensante quæ, a quibus, et quibus temporibus fieri debeant. Eo namque currente et magna spatia transcurrente, illis tanquam veteranis et emeritis interim debebatur otium." — *Materials*, vol. i. p. 290.

them back into the ways of peace. All men, therefore, may come to him and drink without fear, and they shall find salvation, body and soul." [1]

The details of the miracles contain many interesting pictures of old English life. St. Thomas was kind to persons drowned or drowning, kind to prisoners, especially kind to children. He was interested in naval matters — launching vessels from the stocks when the shipwrights could not move them, or saving mariners and fishermen in shipwrecks. According to William of Canterbury, the archbishop in his new condition had a weakness for the married clergy, many miracles being worked by him for a *focaria*. Dead lambs, geese, and pigs were restored to life, to silence Sadducees who doubted the resurrection. In remembrance of his old sporting days, the archbishop would mend the broken wings and legs of hawks which had suffered from the herons. Boys and girls found him always ready to listen to their small distresses. A Suffolk yeoman, William of Ramshott, had invited a party to a feast. A neighbor had made him a present of a cheese, and his little daughter Beatrice had been directed to put it away in a safe place. Beatrice did as she was told, but went to play with her brother Hugh, and forgot what she had done with it. The days went on ; the feast day was near. The children hunted in every corner of the house, but no cheese could be found. The nearest town was far off. They had no money to buy another if they could reach it, and a whipping became sadly probable. An idea struck the little Hugh. "Sister," he said, "I have heard that the blessed Thomas is good and kind. Let us pray to Thomas to help us." They went to their beds, and, as Hugh foretold, the saint came to them in their dreams. "Don't you remember," he said, "the old crock in the back kitchen, where the butter used to be kept?" They sprang up, and all was well.

The original question between the king and the arch-

[1] *Materials,* vol. i. pp. 251, 252.

bishop still agitated men's minds, and was still so far from practical settlement that visions were necessary to convert the impenitent. A knight of the court, who contended for the Constitutions of Clarendon, and continued stubborn, was struck with paralysis. Becket came and bade him observe that the Judge of truth had decided against the king by signs and wonders, and that it was a sin to doubt any further. The knight acknowledged his error. Others were less penetrable. The miracles, it was still said, might be deceptive ; and, true or false, miracles could not alter matters of plain right or wrong. Even women were found who refused to believe ; and a characteristic story is told, in which we catch a glimpse of one of the murderers.

A party of gentlemen were dining at a house in Sussex. Hugh de Morville was in the neighborhood, and while they were sitting at dinner a note was brought in from him asking one of the guests who was an old acquaintance to call and see him. The person to whom the note was addressed read it with signs of horror. When the cause was explained, the lady of the house said, " Is that all ? What is there to be alarmed about ? The priest Thomas is dead : well, why need that trouble us ? The clergy were putting their feet on the necks of us all. The archbishop wanted to be the king's master, and he has not succeeded. Eat your victuals, neighbor, like an honest man." The poor lady expressed what doubtless many were feeling. An example was necessary, and one of her children was at once taken dangerously ill. The county neighbors said it was a judgment ; she was made to confess her sins and carry her child to Canterbury to be cured, where, having been the subject of divine interposition, he was " dedicated to God " and was brought up a monk.

Through the offerings the monastery at Canterbury became enormously rich, and riches produced their natural effect. Giraldus Cambrensis, when he paid a visit there a few years later, found the monks dining more luxuriously

9

than the king. According to Nigellus, the precentor of the
cathedral, their own belief in the wonders which they daily
witnessed was not profound, since in the midst of them
Nigellus could write deliberately, as the excuse for the
prevalent profligacy of churchmen, " that the age of miracles was past." It was observed, and perhaps commented
on, that unless the offerings were handsome the miracles
were often withheld. So obvious was this feature that
William of Canterbury was obliged to apologize for it.
" The question rises," he says, " why the martyr takes such
delight in these donations, being now, as he is, in heaven,
where covetousness can have no place. Some say that the
martyr, when in the body, on the occasion of his going into
exile, borrowed much money, being in need of it for his
fellow exiles, and to make presents at court. Being unable
to repay his creditors in life, he may have been anxious
after death that his debts should be discharged, lest his
good name should suffer. And therefore it may be that all
these kings and princes, knights, bishops, priests, monks,
nuns, all ages and conditions, are inspired by God to come
in such troops and take so many vows on them to grant
pensions and annuities." [1]

There is no occasion to pursue into further details the
history of this extraordinary alliance between religion and
lying, which forced on Europe the most extravagant sacerdotalism by evidence as extravagant as itself. By an appropriate affinity the claims of the Church to spiritual
supremacy were made to rest on falsehood, whether unconscious or deliberate, and when the falsehood ceased to be
credible the system which was based upon it collapsed.
Thus all illusions work at last their own retribution. Ecclesiastical miracles are not worked in vindication of purity of
life or piety of character. They do not intrude themselves
into a presence to which they can lend no increase of beauty
and furnish no additional authority. They are the spurious

[1] *Materials*, vol. i. p. 327.

offspring of the passion of theologians for their own most extravagant assumptions. They are believed, they become the material of an idolatry, till the awakened conscience of the better part of mankind rises at last in revolt, and the fantastic pretensions and the evidence alleged in support of them depart together and cumber the world no more. We return to authentic history.

CHAPTER XII.

WHEN the news of the catastrophe at Canterbury arrived in Normandy, the king was for a time stunned. None knew better than he the temper of his subjects on the present condition of the dispute with the Church. The death of the great disturber was natural, and may, perhaps, have been inevitable. Nevertheless, if the result of it as seemed too likely to be the case, was his own excommunication and an interdict on his dominions, a rebellion in Normandy was certain, and a rebellion in England was only too probable. Firm as might have been his own grasp, his hold on his continental duchies was not strengthened by his English sovereignty. The Norman nobles and prelates saw their country sliding into a province of the island kingdom which their fathers had subdued. If they were to lose their independence, their natural affinity was towards the land with which they were geographically combined. The revolutionary forces were already at work which came to maturity in the next generation, and if Normandy and Anjou were laid under interdict for a crime committed in England and for an English cause, an immediate insurrection might be anticipated with certainty. The state of England was scarcely more satisfactory. The young princes, who had been over-indulged in childhood, were showing symptoms of mutiny. The private relations between an English sovereign and his family were not yet regarded as the property of his subjects; the chroniclers rarely indulged in details of royal scandals, and the dates of Henry's infidelities are vaguely given. Giraldus says that he remained true to his queen till she tempted her sons into rebellion, but Eleanor herself might have told the story differently, and the fire which was about to burst so furiously may have been long smouldering. As to the people generally, it was evident that Becket had a formidable faction among them. The humpbacked Earl of Leicester was dead, but his son, the new earl, was of the same temper as his father. The barons resented the demolition of their castles, which the king had already begun, and the curtailment of their feudal authority. An exasperating inquiry was at that moment going forward into the conduct of the sheriffs. They had levied tax and toll at their pleasure, and the king's interference with them they regarded as an invasion of their liberties. Materials for complaint were lying about in abundance, and anything might be feared if to the injuries of the knights and barons were added the injuries of the Church, and rebellion could be gilded with a show of sanctity. The same spirit which sent them to die under the walls of Acre might prompt them equally to avenge the murder of the archbishop. Henry himself was a representative of his age. He, too, really believed that the clergy were semi-supernatural beings, whose curse it might be dangerous to undergo. The murder itself had been accompanied with every circumstance most calculated to make a profound impression. The sacrilege was something, but the sacrilege was not the worst. Many a bloody scene had been witnessed in that age in church and cathedral; abbots had invaded one another at the head of armed parties; monks had fought and been killed within consecrated walls, and sacred vessels and sacred relics had been carried off among bleeding bodies. High dignitaries were occasionally poisoned in the sacramental wine, and such a crime, though serious, was not regarded as exceptionally dreadful. But Becket had but just returned to England after a formal reconciliation in the presence of all Europe. The King of France, the Count of Flanders, and the Count of Blois had pledged their words for his safety. He had been killed in his own cathedral. He had fallen with a dignity, and even grandeur, which his bitterest enemies were obliged to admire. The murderers were Henry's own immediate attendants, and Henry could not deny that he had himself used words which they might construe into a sanction of what they had done.

Giraldus Cambrensis, who when young had seen and spoken with him, has left us a sketch of Henry the Second's appearance and character more than usually distinct. Henry was of middle height, with a thick short neck and a square chest. His body was stout and fleshy, his arms sinewy and long. His head was round and large, his hair and beard reddish-brown, his complexion florid, his eyes gray, with fire glowing at the bottom of them. His habits were exceptionally temperate; he ate little, drank little, and was always extremely active. He was on horseback, at dawn, either hunting or else on business. When off his horse he was on his feet, and rarely sat down till supper time. He was easy of approach, gracious, pleasant, and in conversation remarkably agreeable. Notwithstanding his outdoor habits he had read largely, and his memory was extremely tenacious. It was said of him, that he never forgot a face which he had once seen, or a thing which he had heard or read that was worth remembering. He was pious too, Giraldus says, *pietate spectabilis.* The piety unfortunately, in Giraldus's eyes, took the wrong shape of an over-zeal for justice, which brought him into his trouble with the Church, while to his technical "religious duties" he was less attentive than he ought to have been. He allowed but an hour a day for mass, and while mass was being said he usually thought of something else. To the poor he was profusely charitable, "filling the hungry with good things, and sending the rich empty away." He was *largus in publico, parvus in privato;* he spent freely in the public service and little on himself. As a statesman he was reserved, seldom showing his own thoughts. He was a good judge of character, rarely changing an opinion of a man which he had once formed. He was patient of opposition, and trusted much to time to find his way through difficulties. In war he was dangerous from his energy and his intellect. But he had no love for war, he was essentially a friend of peace, and after a battle could not control his emotion at the loss of his men. "In short," Giraldus concludes, "if God had but elected him to grace and converted him to a right understanding of the privileges of his Church, he would have been an incomparable prince."[1] Such was Henry, the first of the English Plantagenet kings, a man whose faults it is easy to blame, whose many excellences it would have been less easy to imitate — a man of whom may be said what can be affirmed but rarely of any mortal, that the more clearly his history is known the more his errors will be forgiven, the more we shall find to honor and admire.

He was at Argenteuil when the fatal account was brought to him. He shut himself in his room, ate nothing for three days, and for five weeks remained in penitential seclusion. Time was precious, for his enemies were not asleep. Lewis and the Archbishop of Sens wrote passionately to the pope, charging the king with the guilt of the murder, and insisting that so enormous an outrage should be punished at once and with the utmost severity. The Archbishop of Sens, on his own authority as legate, laid Normandy under interdict, and Alexander, startled into energy at last, sent persons to the spot to confirm the archbishop's action, and to extend the censures over England. Henry roused himself at last. He dispatched the Archbishop of Rouen and two other bishops[2] to explain what had happened, so far as explanation was possible ; and as the danger was pressing and bishops travelled slowly, three other churchmen, the Abbot

---

[1] Giraldus, vol. v. p. 301, etc.

[2] The Bishop of Worcester was one of them. The Bishop of Worcester could explain to the pope why his inhibitory letter on the coronation had never been delivered in England.

of Valaise and the Archdeacons of Lisieux and Salisbury, pushed on before them. On their first arrival these envoys were refused an audience. When they were admitted to Alexander's presence at last, the attempt at palliation was listened to with horror. Two of Becket's clergy were at the papal court, and had possession of pope and cardinals, and it appeared only too likely that at the approaching Easter Alexander himself would declare Henry excommunicated. By private negotiations with some of the cardinals they were able to delay the sentence till the coming of the bishops. The bishops brought them a promise on Henry's part to submit to any penance which the pope might enjoin, and to acquiesce in any order which the pope might prescribe for the government of the clergy. An immediate catastrophe was thus averted. Cardinals Albert and Theodoric were commissioned at leisure to repair to Normandy and do what might be found necessary. To the mortification of Lewis the censures were meanwhile suspended, and the interdict pronounced by the Archbishop of Sens was not confirmed.

Henry on his part prepared to deserve the pope's forgiveness. Uncertain what Alexander might resolve upon, he returned to England as soon as he had recovered his energy. He renewed the orders at the ports against the admission of strangers and against the introduction of briefs from Rome, which might disturb the public peace. He then at once undertook a duty which long before had been enjoined upon him by Alexander's predecessor, and had been left too long neglected.

Ireland had been converted to the Christian faith by an apostle from the Holy See, but in seven centuries the Irish Church had degenerated from its original purity. Customs had crept in unknown in other Latin communions, and savoring of schism. No regular communication had been maintained with the authorities at Rome; no confirmation of abbots and bishops had been applied for or paid for. At a council held in 1151 a papal legate had been present, and an arrangement had been made for the presentation of the palls of the four Irish archbishoprics. But the legate's general account of the state of Irish affairs increased the pope's anxiety for more vigorous measures. Not only Peter's pence and first fruits were not paid to himself—not only tithes were not paid to the clergy—but the most sacred rites were perverted or neglected. In parts of the island children were not baptized at all. Where baptism was observed, it more resembled a magical ceremony than a sacrament of the Church. Any person who happened to be present at a birth dipped the child three times in water or milk, without security for the use of the appointed words. Marriage scarcely could be said to exist. An Irish chief took as many wives as he pleased, and paid no respect to degrees of consanguinity.[1] Even incest was not uncommon[2] among them. The clergy, though not immoral in the technical sense, were hard drinkers. The bishops lived in religious houses, and preferred a quiet life to interfering with lawlessness and violence. The people of Ireland, according to Giraldus, who was sent over to study their character, were bloodthirsty savages, and strangers who settled among them caught their habits by an irresistible instinct. But Ireland, religious Ireland especially, had something in its history which commanded respect and interest. A thousand saints had printed their names and memories on Irish soil. St. Patrick and St. Bride had worked more miracles than even the water of St. Thomas. Apostles from Ireland had carried the Christian faith into Scotland, into Iceland, and into Scandinavia.

The popes felt the exclusion of so singular a country from the Catholic commonwealth to be a scandal which ought no longer to be acquiesced in. In 1155 Pope Adrian

---

[1] "Plerique enim illorum quot volebant uxores habebant, et etiam cognatas suas germanas habere solebant sibi uxores."—Benedict, vol. i. p. 28.

[2] "Non incestus vitant."—Giraldus Cambrensis, vol. v. p. 138.

had laid before Henry the Second the duty imposed on
Christian princes to extend the truth among barbarous
nations, to eradicate vice, and to secure Peter's pence to
the Holy See; and a bull had been issued, sanctioning and
enjoining the conquest of Ireland.[1]

Busy with more pressing concerns, Henry had put off
the expedition from year to year. Meanwhile, the Irish
chiefs and kings were quarrelling among themselves.
MacMorrough of Leinster was driven out, and had come to
England for help. The king hesitated in his answer; but
volunteers had been found for the service in Sir Robert
Fitzstephen, Sir Maurice Prendergast, Sir Maurice Fitz-
gerald, Earl Richard Strigul, with other knights and gentlemen who were eager for adventure; and a Norman
occupation had been made good along the eastern coast of
Munster and Leinster. The invasion had been undertaken
without the king's consent. He had affected to regard it
with disapproval; and the Irish of the west, rallying from
their first panic, were collecting in force to drive the intruders into the sea. The desirableness of doing something
to entitle him to the pope's gratitude, the convenience of
absence from home at a time when dangerous notices might
be served upon him, and the certainty that Alexander would
hesitate to pronounce him excommunicated when engaged
in a conquest which, being undertaken under a papal sanc-

---

[1] Irish Catholic historians pretend that the bull was a Norman forgery.
The bull was alleged to have been granted in 1155: in 1170 it was acted
upon. In 1171–72 a council was held at Cashel, in which the reforms demanded by Pope Adrian were adopted, and the Irish Church was remod-
elled, and a report of the proceedings was forwarded to Alexander the
Third. In 1174 a confirmation of the original bull was published, profess-
ing to have been signed by Alexander. In 1177 Cardinal Vivian came
as legate from Rome, who, in a synod at Dublin, declared formally in the
pope's name that the sovereignty of Ireland was vested in the English
king, and enjoined the Irish to submit *sub pœná anathematis.* It requires
some hardihood to maintain in the face of these undisputed facts that the
pope was kept in ignorance that the island had been invaded and conquered under a sanction doubly forged, and that Cardinal Vivian was
either a party to the fraud, or that when in Ireland he never discovered it.

tion, resembled a crusade, determined Henry to use the opportunity, and at last accomplish the mission which Adrian had imposed upon him. After his return from Normandy, he passed rapidly through England. He collected a fleet at Milford Haven, and landed at Waterford on October 18, 1171. All Ireland, except the north, at once submitted. The king spent the winter in Dublin in a palace of wattles, the best lodging which the country could afford. In the spring he was able to report to Alexander that the obnoxious customs were abolished, that Catholic discipline had been introduced, and that the Irish tribute would be thenceforward punctually remitted to the papal treasury.

Could he have remained in Ireland for another year, the conquest would have been completed; but in April he was recalled to meet the two cardinals who had arrived in Normandy to receive his submission for Becket's death. The Irish annexation was of course a service which was permitted to be counted in his favor, but the circumstances of the murder, and Henry's conduct in connection with it, both before and after, still required an appearance of scrutiny. Not the least remarkable feature in the story is that the four knights had not been punished. They had not been even arrested. They had gone together, after leaving Canterbury, to De Morville's Castle of Knaresborough. They had been excommunicated, but they had received no further molestation. It has been conjectured that they owed their impunity to Becket's own claim for the exclusive jurisdiction of the spiritual courts in cases where spiritual persons were concerned. But the wildest advocates of the immunities of the Church had never dreamed of protecting laymen who had laid their hands on clerks. The explanation was that the king had acted honorably by taking the responsibility on himself, and had not condescended to shield his own reputation by the execution of men whose fault had been over-loyalty to himself. Elizabeth might have remembered with advantage the example of her ancestor when she punished Davison, under circumstances not wholly dissimilar, for the execution of the Queen of Scots.

The king met the cardinals at Caen in the middle of May. At the first interview the difficulty was disposed of which was most immediately pressing, and arrangements were made for a repetition of the ceremony which had been the occasion of the excommunication of the bishops. Prince Henry and the Princess Margaret were again crowned at Winchester on the 27th of August by the Archbishop of Rouen and the Bishops of Evreux and Worcester, the same prelates who had gone on the mission to Rome. At Avranches on the 27th of September, at a second and more solemn assembly, the king confessed his guilt for the archbishop's death. He had not desired it, he said, and it had caused him the deepest sorrow; but he admitted that he had used words which the knights had naturally misconstrued. He attempted no palliation, and declared himself willing to endure any penalty which the cardinals might be pleased to impose.

The conditions with which the cardinals were satisfied implied an admission that in the original quarrel the right had lain with the king. All the miracles at Canterbury had made no difference in this essential point. The king promised to continue his support to Alexander as long as Alexander continued to recognize him as a Catholic sovereign — as long, that is, as he did not excommunicate him. He promised not to interfere with appeals to Rome in ecclesiastical causes, but with the reservation that if he had ground for suspecting an invasion of the rights of the crown, he might take measures to protect himself. He promised to abandon any customs complained of by the Church which had been introduced in his own reign; but such customs, he said, would be found to be few or none. He pardoned Becket's friends; he restored the privileges and the estates of the see of Canterbury. For himself, he took

the cross, with a vow to serve for three years in the Holy
Land, unless the pope perceived that his presence was
needed elsewhere. Meanwhile he promised to maintain
two hundred Templars there for a year.

On these terms Henry was absolved. Geoffrey Ridel and
John of Oxford, Becket's active opponents, whom he had
twice cursed, were promoted to bishoprics. The four knights
must have been absolved also, since they returned to the
court, and, like their master, took the vows as Crusaders.
The monastic chroniclers consign them to an early and
miserable death. The industry of Dean Stanley has discovered them, two years after the murder, to have been
again in attendance on the sovereign. Tracy became Justiciary of Normandy, and was at Falaise in 1174, when
William the Lion did homage to Henry. De Morville,
after a year's suspension, became again Justiciary of Northumberland. Fitzurse apparently chose Ireland as the
scene of his penance. A Fitzurse was in the second flight
of Norman invaders, and was the founder of a family known
to later history as the MacMahons, the Irish equivalent of
the Son of the Bear.

But Henry was not yet delivered from the consequences
of his contest with Becket, and the conspiracy which had
been formed against him under the shelter of Becket's name
was not to be dissolved by the spell of a papal absolution.
Lewis of France had taken up Becket's cause, not that
felonious clerks might go unhanged, but that an English
king might not divide his own land with him. The Earl
of Leicester had torn down Reginald of Cologne's altars,
not alone because he was an orthodox Catholic, but that,
with the help of an ambitious ecclesiasticism, he might
break the power of the crown. Through France, through
England, through Normandy, a combination had been
formed for Henry's humiliation, and although the pope no
longer sanctioned it, the purpose was deeply laid, and could
not lightly be surrendered.

Unable to strike at his rival as a spiritual outlaw, Lewis found a point where he was no less vulnerable in the jealousy of his queen and the ambition and pride of his sons. His aim was to separate England from its French dependencies. He, and perhaps Eleanor, instigated Prince Henry to demand after the second coronation that his father should divide his dominions, and make over one part or the other to him as an independent sovereign. The king of course refused. Prince Henry and his wife escaped to Lewis *per consilium comitum et baronum Angliæ et Normanniæ qui patrem suum odio habebant.*[1] The younger princes, Richard and Geoffrey, followed them; and a council was held at Paris, where the Count of Flanders the Count of Boulogne, William the Lion, and the Earl of Huntingdon from Scotland, and the English and Norman disaffected nobles, combined with Lewis for a general attack upon the English king. England was to rise. Normandy was to rise. William was to invade Northumberland. The Count of Flanders was to assist the English insurgents in the eastern counties. Lewis himself was to lead an army into Normandy, where half the barons and bishops were ready to join him. The three English princes, embittered, it may be, by their mother's injuries, swore to make no peace with their father without consent of their allies.

For a time it seemed as if Henry must be overwhelmed. Open enemies were on all sides of him. Of his professed friends too many were disloyal at heart. The Canterbury frenzy added fuel to the conflagration by bringing God into the field. The Earl of Norfolk and Lord Ferrars rose in East Anglia. Lewis and young Henry crossed the frontier into Normandy. The Scots poured over the Tweed into Northumberland. Ireland caught the contagion uninvited; the greater part of the force which had remained there was recalled, and only a few garrisons were left. Had Alexander allowed the Church to lend its help, the

[1] Benedict.

king must have fallen; but Alexander honorably adhered to his engagement at Avranches.

The king himself remained on the continent, struggling as he best could against war and treason. Chief Justice de Luci and Humfrey de Bohun faced the Scots beyond Newcastle, and drove them back to Berwick. In the midst of their success they learned that the Earl of Leicester had landed in Norfolk with an army of Flemings. They left the north to its fate. They flew back. Lord Arundel joined them, and the old Earl of Cornwall, who befriended Becket while he could, but had no sympathies with rebellion. They fell on the Flemings near Bury St. Edmunds, and flung them into total wreck. Ten thousand were killed. Leicester himself and the rest were taken, and scarce a man escaped to carry back the news to Gravelines.[1]

The victory in Norfolk was the first break in the cloud. The rebellion in England had its back broken, and waverers began to doubt, in spite of the miracles, whether God was on its side. Bad news, however, came from the north. The Scots flowed back, laying waste Cumberland and Northumberland with wild ferocity. At the opening of the summer of 1174 another army of French, Flemings, and insurgent English was collected at Gravelines to revenge the defeat at Bury, and this time the Earl of Flanders and Prince Henry were to come in person at the head of it.

An invasion so lead and countenanced could only be resisted by the king in person. The barons had sworn allegiance to the prince, and the more loyal of them might be uncertain in what direction their duties lay. Sad and stern, prepared for the worst, yet resolute to contend to the last against the unnatural coalition, Henry crossed in July to Southampton; but, before repairing to London to collect his forces, he turned aside out of his road for a singular and touching purpose.

[1] October 16, 1173.

Although the conspiracy against which he was fighting was condemned by the pope it had grown nevertheless too evidently out of the contest with Becket, which had ended so terribly. The combination of his wife and sons with his other enemies was something off the course of nature — strange, dark, and horrible. He was abler than most of his contemporaries, but his piety was (as with most wise men) a check upon his intellect. He, it is clear, did not share in the suspicion that the miracles at the archbishop's tomb were the work either of fraud or enchantment. He was not a person who for political reasons would affect emotions which he despised. He had been Becket's friend. Becket had been killed, in part at least, through his own fault; and, though he might still believe himself to have been essentially right in the quarrel, the miracles showed that the archbishop had been really a saint. A more complete expiation than the pope had enjoined might be necessary before the avenging spirit, too manifestly at work, could be pacified.

From Southampton he directed his way to Canterbury, where the bishops had been ordered to meet him. He made offerings at the various churches which he passed on his way. On reaching Harbledown, outside the city, he alighted at the Chapel of St. Nicholas, and thence went [1] on foot to St. Dunstan's Oratory, adjoining the wall. At the oratory he stripped off his usual dress. He put on a hair penitential shirt, over which a coarse pilgrim's cloak was thrown; and in this costume, with bare and soon bleeding feet, Henry, King of England, Lord of Ireland. Duke of Normandy, and Count of Anjou, walked through the streets to the cathedral. Pausing at the spot where the archbishop had fallen, and kissing the stone, he descended into the crypt to the tomb, burst into tears, and flung himself on the ground. There, surrounded by a group of bishops, knights, and monks, he remained long upon his knees in silent

[1] July 12.

prayer. The Bishop of London said for him, what he had said at Avranches, that he had not commanded the murder, but had occasioned it by his hasty words. When the bishop ended, he rose, and repeated his confession with his own lips. He had caused the archbishop's death; therefore he had come in person to acknowledge his sin, and to entreat the brothers of the monastery to pray for him.

At the tomb he offered rich silks and wedges of gold. To the chapter he gave lands. For himself he vowed to erect and endow a religious house, which should be dedicated to St. Thomas. Thus amply, in the opinion of the monks, *reconciliari meruit,* he deserved to be forgiven. But the satisfaction was still incomplete. The martyr's injuries, he said, must be avenged on his own person. He threw off his cloak, knelt again, and laid his head upon the tomb. Each bishop and abbot present struck him five times with a whip. Each one of the eighty monks struck him thrice. Strange scene! None can be found more characteristic of the age; none more characteristic of Henry Plantagenet.

The penance done, he rose and resumed his cloak; and there by the tomb through the remainder of the July day, and through the night till morning, he remained silently sitting, without food or sleep. The cathedral doors were left open by his orders. The people of the city came freely to gape and stare at the singular spectacle. There was the terrible King Henry, who had sent the knights to kill their archbishop, sitting now in dust and ashes. The most ingenious cunning could not have devised a better method of winning back the affection of his subjects; yet with no act of king or statesman had ingenious cunning ever less to do. In the morning he heard mass, and presented offerings at the various altars. Then he became king once more, and rode to London to prepare for the invader. If his humiliation was an act of vain superstition, Providence encouraged him in his weakness. On the day which followed it William

10

the Lion was defeated and made prisoner at Alnwick. A week later came news that the army at Gravelines had dissolved, and that the invasion was abandoned. Delivered from peril at home, Henry flew back to France and flung Lewis back over his own frontier. St. Thomas was now supposed to be fighting for King Henry. Imagination becomes reality when it gives to one party certainty of victory, to the other the anticipation of defeat. By the spring of 1175 the great combination was dissolved. The princes returned to their duty; the English and Norman rebels to their allegiance; and with Alexander's mediation Henry and Lewis and the Count of Flanders were for a time once more reconciled.

re less respectful to
˘ decreẽs.
ᵕnd Walter of
ᵕleading the
ᵕnishing
ᵕerce-
ᵕs

CHAPTER XIII.

THOUGH the formal canonization of Becket could not b̥
accomplished with the speed which his impatient friends
demanded, it was declared with the least delay which the
necessary forms required. A commission which was sent
from Rome to inquire into the authenticity of the miracles
having reported satisfactorily, the promotion of the archbishop was immediately decreed, and the monks were able
to pray to him without fear of possible irregularity. Due
honor having been thus paid to the Church's champion, it
became possible to take up again the ever-pressing problem
of the Church's reform.

Between the pope and the king there had never really
been much difference of opinion. They were now able to
work harmoniously together. A successor for Becket at
Canterbury was found in the Prior of Dover, for whose
good sense we have a sufficient guarantee in the abhorrence
with which he was regarded by the ardent champions of
Church supremacy. The reformation was commenced in
Normandy. After the ceremony at Avranches the cardinals
who had come from Rome to receive Henry's confession held
a council there. The resolutions arrived at show that the
picture of the condition of the clergy left to us by Nigellus
is not really overdrawn. It was decided that children were
to be no more admitted to the cure of souls — a sufficient
proof that children had been so admitted. It was decided
that the sons of priests should not succeed to their father's
preferments — an evidence not only of the habits of the
incumbents, but of the tendency of Church benefices to become hereditary. Yet more significantly the guilty bargains

the Lion was defeat which benefices were let out to farm,
week later came presented incumbents on condition of shar-
dissolved, and bry money ; while pluralist ecclesiastics, of
from peril act himself had been a conspicuous instance, were
Lewis ba; give a third, at least, of their tithes to the vicars.
suppose close of the war, in 1175, a similar council was held
com Westminster under the new primate. Not only the
tAvranches resolutions were adopted there, but indications
appeared that among the English clergy simony and license
were at a yet grosser point than on the Continent. Benefices had been publicly set up to sale. The religious houses
received money for the admission of monks and nuns.
Priests, and even bishops, had demanded fees for the administration of the sacraments ; while as regarded manners
and morals, it was evident that the priestly character sat
lightly on the secular clergy. They carried arms ; they
wore their hair long like laymen ; they frequented taverns
and more questionable places ; the more reputable among
them were sheriffs and magistrates. So far as decrees of a
council could alter the inveterate habits of the order, a
better state of things was attempted to be instituted. In
the October following, Cardinal Hugezun came from Rome
to arrange the vexed question of the liability of clerks to
trial in the civil courts. The customs for which Henry
pleaded seem at that time to been substantially recognized.
Offenders were degraded by their ordinaries and passed
over to the secular judges. For one particular class of
offences definite statutory powers were conceded to the
State. The clergy were notorious violators of the forest
laws. Deer-stealing implied a readiness to commit other
crimes, and Cardinal Hugezun formally consented that orders should be no protection in such cases. The betrayal
of their interests on a matter which touched so nearly the
occupation of their lives was received by the clergy with a
scream of indignation. Their language on the occasion is
an illustration of what may have been observed often, be-

fore and since, that no order of men are less respectful to spiritual authority when they disapprove its decrees.

"The aforesaid cardinal," wrote Benedict and Walter of Coventry, "conceded to the king the right of impleading the clerks of his realm under the forest laws, and of punishing them for taking deer. Limb of Satan that he was! mercenary satellite of the devil himself! Of a shepherd he was made a robber. Seeing the wolf coming, he fled away and left the sheep whom the supreme pontiff had committed to his charge." [1]

The angry advocates of ecclesiastical license might have spared their passion. The laws of any country cannot be maintained above the level of the average intelligence of the people; and in another generation the clergy would be free to carry their cross-bows without danger of worse consequences than a broken crown from the staff of a gamekeeper. "Archbishop Richard," says Giraldus, "basely surrendered the rights which the martyr Thomas had fought for and won, but Archbishop Stephen recovered them." The blood of St. Thomas had not been shed, and the martyr of Canterbury had not been allowed a monopoly of wonder-working, that a priest should be forbidden to help himself to a haunch of vension on festival days. In the great Charter of English freedom the liberties of the Church were comprehended in the form, or almost in the form, in which Becket himself would have defined them. The barons paid for the support of the clergy on that memorable occasion by the concession of their most extravagant demands. Benefit of clergy thenceforward was permitted to throw an enchanted shield, not round deer-stealers only, but round thieves and murderers, and finally round every villain that could read. The spiritual courts, under the name of liberty, were allowed to develop a system of tyranny and corrup-

---

[1] "Ecce membrum Satanæ! ecce ipsius Satanæ conductus satelles! qui tam subito factus de pastore raptor videns lupum venientem fugit et dimisit oves sibi a summo pontifice commissas."

tion unparalleled in the administrative annals of any time or country. The English laity were for three centuries condemned to writhe under the yoke which their own credulous folly had imposed on them, till the spirit of Henry the Second at length revived, and the aged iniquity was brought to judgment at the Reformation.

Prices and Styles of the Different Editions

OF

FROUDE'S HISTORY OF ENGLAND.

The Chelsea Edition.

In half roan, gilt top, per set of twelve vols. 12mo... ....$21.00

Elegance and cheapness are combined in a remarkable degree in this edition. It takes its name from the place of Mr. Froude's residence in London, also famous as the home of Thomas Carlyle.

The Popular Edition.

In cloth, at the rate of $1.25 per volume. The set (12 vols.), in a neat box.$15.00
The Same in half calf extra... 36.00

This edition is printed from the same plates as the other editions, and on firm, white paper. It is, without exception, the cheapest set of books of its class ever issued in this country.

The Library Edition.

In twelve vols. crown 8vo, cloth............... ....$30.00
The Same, in half calf extra... 50.00

The Edition is printed on laid and tinted paper, at the Riverside Press, and is in every respect worthy a place in the most carefully selected library.

SHORT STUDIES ON GREAT SUBJECTS.

By JAMES ANTHONY FROUDE, M.A.,
Author of "History of England," "The English in Ireland during the Eighteenth Century," etc.

POPULAR EDITION. Three vols. 12mo, cloth, $1.50 per vol. The Set....$4.50
CHELSEA EDITION. Three vols. 12mo, half roan, gilt top, $2.00 per volume. Per Set... 6.00

The Complete Works of James Anthony Froude, M.A.

HISTORY OF ENGLAND AND SHORT STUDIES.
Fifteen vols., in a neat Box.

POPULAR EDITION... ...$19.50
CHELSEA EDITION... 27.00

The above works sent, post-paid, by the publishers, on receipt of the price

SCRIBNER, ARMSTRONG & CO.,

NEW YORK

www.ingramcontent.com/pod-product-compliance
Lightning Source LLC
Chambersburg PA
CBHW021116020726
47500CB00003B/784